THE GLADDY GOLD MYSTERIES

"This is one sassy and smart series with a colorful gang of senior sleuths." —*Mystery Scene*

"Beyond the skillful blend of Yiddish humor, affectionate characters and serious undercurrents... picks up speed and flavor with some **twists worthy of Agatha Christie's archetypal dame detective, Miss Marple.**" —*Publishers Weekly*

"What gives the book its warmth is the way Lakin has turned this group of friends into a family who are there not only for the fun and laughter but also for the heartbreak and tears." —*Romantic Times*

"**Young and old, Jewish, Protestant, atheist, all will love this tale** told with clarity, wit and interesting characters. This is a must-read-mystery." —iloveamysterynewsletter.com

"Rita Lakin shows a real flair for comic mysteries.... **The plotting is expert, but the background color of life among older retired people is wonderful** (and sometimes very poignant)." —*Connecticut Post* Forum

"This is a **funny, warm, absolutely delightful** tale... a must read." —*Mysterious Women*

Getting Old Is
To Die For

Rita Lakin

A DELL BOOK

GETTING OLD IS TO DIE FOR
A Dell Book / January 2008

Published by Bantam Dell
A Division of Random House, Inc.
New York, New York

This is a work of fiction. Names, characters, places, and incidents either are the product of the author's imagination or are used fictitiously. Any resemblance to actual persons, living or dead, events, or locales is entirely coincidental.

Dell is a registered trademark of Random House, Inc., and the colophon is a trademark of Random House, Inc.

ISBN 978-0-440-24387-8

Printed in the United States of America
Published simultaneously in Canada

www.bantamdell.com

OPM   10 9 8 7 6 5 4 3 2 1

This book is for James
with Love
from his Grandma

Introduction
to Our Characters

GLADDY & HER GLADIATORS

Gladys (Gladdy) Gold, 75 Our heroine and her funny, adorable, and sometimes impossible partners:

Evelyn (Evvie) Markowitz, 73 Gladdy's sister. Logical, a regular Sherlock Holmes

Ida Franz, 71 Stubborn, mean, great for in-your-face confrontation

Bella Fox, 83 The "shadow." She's so forgettable, she's perfect for surveillance, but smarter than you think

Sophie Meyerbeer, 80 Master of disguises, she lives for color-coordination

YENTAS, KIBITZERS, SUFFERERS: THE INHABITANTS OF PHASE TWO

Hy Binder, 88 A man of a thousand jokes, all of them tasteless

Lola Binder, 78 His wife, who hasn't a thought in her head that he hasn't put there

Denny Ryan, 42 The handyman. Sweet, kind, mentally slow

Enya Slovak, 84 Survivor of "the camps" but never really survived

Tessie Hoffman, 56 Chubby, recently married to Sol Spankowitz

Millie Weiss, 85 Suffering with Alzheimer's

Irving Weiss, 86 Suffering because she's suffering

Mary Mueller, 60 Neighbor and nurse, whose husband left her

ODDBALLS AND FRUITCAKES

The Canadians, 30–40-ish Young, tan, and clueless
Sol Spankowitz, 79 Reluctant husband
Dora Dooley, 81 Jack's neighbor, loves soap operas

THE COP AND THE COP'S POP

Morgan (Morrie) Langford, 35 Tall, lanky, sweet, and smart
Jack Langford, 75 Handsome and romantic

THE LIBRARY MAVEN

Conchetta Aguilar, 38 Her Cuban coffee could grow hair on your chest

NEW TENANTS

Barbi Stevens, 20-ish, and *Casey Wright, 30-ish* Cousins who moved from California

AND

Yolanda Diaz, 22 Her English is bad, but her heart is good

NEW YORK CHARACTERS
GLADDY'S FAMILY

Emily Levinson, 46
Dr. Alan Levinson, 50
Elizabeth, 21
Erin, 19

Lindsay, 11
Patrick, 15

JACK'S FAMILY
Lisa Berman, 44
Dan Berman, 46
Jeffrey, 13
Jeremy, 11
Molly, 3 months old

EVVIE'S FAMILY

Joe Markowitz, 77 Evvie's ex-husband
Martha Evans, 48
Elliot Evans, 49

Gladdy's Glossary

Yiddish (meaning Jewish) came into being between the ninth and twelfth centuries in Germany as an adaptation of German dialect to the special uses of Jewish religious life.

In the early twentieth century, Yiddish was spoken by eleven million Jews in Eastern Europe and the United States. Its use declined radically. However, lately there has been a renewed interest in embracing Yiddish once again as a connection to Jewish culture.

b'shert	fate
chutzpah	gumption
halvah	pastry
kvell	glow with pride
nu	so? or well?
oy	oh no (disgust; frustration)
schlemiel	a loser
shmattes	rags; old garments
tuckus	rear end

"Don't Call Them Old, Call Them . . ."

Words like "Senior," "Elderly," and "Old" are out.
Nearly four thousand seniors responded to a survey
as to how they would like to be addressed.
Celebrities like Quincy Jones, 73, responded
with "The Silver Foxes." Judge Judy, 63, offered
"The Better-Than-Evers."

Write-in selections, to name just a few:
"Seasoned Citizens"
"Geri-Actives"
"Bonus Years"
"Sage Age"
"XYZ Group" (extra years of zest)
"Third Half"
"Melders" (combining middle age with elders)
"Rewirement" (not retirement)

Alan Brown, 66, of Plantation, Florida, perhaps
said it best and funniest. "Metallic Stage. For the
silver in your hair, the gold in your teeth, the tin ear
you're developing, the platinum credit card you're
being offered, the titanium implant in your hip and
the lead in your behind."
—*From the article by David Oliver Relin in* Parade
  *magazine, March 2006, cosponsored also by the
  Harvard School of Public Health and the MetLife
  Foundation*

Getting Old Is
To Die For

NEW YEAR'S EVE 1961

RIVERSIDE DRIVE, NEW YORK CITY

*I*t's not even midnight and they're celebrating already. What about my celebration?" Emily Gold, eleven years old today, four hours and fifteen minutes away from the actual moment she was born, was doing her own countdown. "Five minutes later my birthday would have been on January first. In the next year."

"Mmm." Gladdy made agreeing, reassuring sounds as she took the icing out of the fridge. She knew those facts continued to awe her adorable daughter; recounting them had become her last-day-of-the-year ritual.

Emily leaned out the window as far as she could. The apartment's fourth-story fire escape blocked her view, so she kept wiggling for a better look. "You should see those people down there *hanging on to one another. They're blowing horns and wearing funny hats. But I still don't see Daddy."*

She pretended to pout, but Gladdy knew how excited her daughter really was. Emily would never admit that she liked having her birthday on the biggest, most exciting night of the year. She blew her breath out, showing her mom the wispy cloud it made.

"Close that window! It's already freezing in here." Gladdy shivered despite the fact she wore two sweaters over her brown woolen dress. Damn that landlord of theirs. He only allowed the super to heat up the radiator twice a day, for one hour at a time. Twelve stories high, six apartments on each floor, and nobody ever listened to the tenants' complaints. What a harsh winter this had been. And living near the Hudson River with its frigid winds only made it worse. She wished it were spring. Winters always depressed her, with the icy brilliance of the sun and the oppressively long black nights.

Emily pulled herself inside and shut the window.

Gladdy shivered again, but it wasn't from the cold. She hugged herself and looked at the clock. She, too, wished Jack would get home. Their neighborhood, even the area around the university where Jack taught English, was becoming unsafe. Drugs were starting to be a problem. She didn't like her husband coming home in the dark.

"Don't you want to help me decorate your

cake?" She picked up a spatula and beckoned Emily, who joined her at their red Formica and chrome kitchen table.

Emily's long brown hair was damp and stringy from the night air and she shook it wildly, laughing as she did. She took the spatula from her mother and continued the smooth flat layering of the icing.

"Do you think you'll ever pick another kind of cake on one of your birthdays?" Gladdy asked.

"No, never. Chocolate and vanilla's always gonna be my favorite."

The older her daughter got, the more they looked alike. Same oval face, same greenish-gray eyes. Same straight hair that refused to curl. Emily was tall for her age and lanky, the way Gladdy had been at her age. No one ever doubted they were mother and child.

"Tell me again why I was born on New Year's Eve."

Gladdy leaned over and kissed Emily's forehead. "You ask that every single year."

"And you always give me the same silly explanation. I can't believe you planned it that way."

Gladdy smiled. "You were my New Year's Eve present for your daddy."

"When I grow up no one will ever remember my birthday. My friends will all be too busy drinking champagne and making silly resolutions."

"Don't worry. There's no way they can forget

this date, nor would they ever forget someone as wonderful as you." She reached out and gently wiped a bit of chocolate off Emily's cheek.

The icing finished, the eleven candles placed carefully with the extra one to grow on, Emily raced to the window again. "What's taking Daddy so long?"

"He'll be here soon. He needs to finish the revisions on his textbook." Gladdy felt a twinge of guilt saying that, when at breakfast that morning she'd chided Jack for the very same thing. In fact, she remembered ruefully, they quarreled about his being late for his child's party. Something they rarely ever did.

"Nobody has to work on New Year's Eve." Emily pouted. "And where's Aunt Evvie and Uncle Joe and Cousin Martha? Even they're late."

Gladdy smiled. Emily may have her mother's looks but she sure has her aunt's impatient disposition and endless energy. *"Well, I'm sure they're walking carefully, so they don't fall on the slippery ice."*

"I'll bet they get me the same present. Every year another Barbie doll. Don't they know I'm too old for that?" Emily hoisted herself onto the red kitchen counter and dangled her legs. "And you and Daddy will give me books again."

"You love to read."

"Of course I do. I just want to be surprised sometime."

"Remember what your daddy says about books?"

"Yes, I do." She mimicked, " 'Books are the windows of the soul. With books you'll never be lonely.' "

She jumped down and raced to the window, opening it again. "I think I see Daddy coming. I recognize how he swings his briefcase. Now my party can start."

Gladdy smiled and walked over to the window to join Emily. Jack always waved to them before he came up. She didn't want to miss it. She reached out and gently guided a wisp of Emily's hair behind her ear.

Jack had named their daughter after the poet Emily Dickinson, hoping his beautiful child might one day be a poet, too.

Suddenly a Dickinson quote popped into Gladdy's head.

Because I could not stop for Death,
He kindly stopped for me—

It was then she heard the scream.

1

TWO LOST SOULS

It's nine-fifteen A.M. My sister, Evvie, who is seventy-three to my seventy-five, sits in my tiny kitchen in her bathing suit drinking coffee. Our towels are draped around our shoulders since the air conditioning is turned up high. September weather here in Fort Lauderdale has been especially hot. We aren't saying much because by now we are talked out. The phone rings. Evvie sighs.

"What do I tell them this time?" I ask as I match her sigh for sigh.

"Same as you did last time. We'll be down when we get there. Let them splash around 'til then."

I answer the phone. This time it's Sophie. I guess the girls are taking turns. "I know we're late," I tell her before she can say a word.

She speaks so loud, I have to hold the receiver away from my ear. "Soon everyone will leave."

"Good," Evvie whispers.

"They're still waiting for you," I report to her.

"That's exactly why I'm up here, instead of down at the pool. If I stall long enough they'll go home."

I hold out the phone to her. "You want to tell Sophie?"

"No. You handle it."

"We're on our way," I lie.

"You've got to face them sometime," I tell Evvie, hanging up the phone.

"Later, better than sooner."

I walk over and pull her out of the chair. "Enough. Come on. You've got to get on with your life."

Evvie laughs bitterly. "Gladdy, that's what I keep telling you."

Neither one of us is in great emotional shape. Evvie can't pull herself together since her tragic love affair with Philip Smythe ended, and I'm not in great shape, either, thanks to Jack acting like a yo-yo. Here today, gone tomorrow. I'm still upset that my boyfriend—the second Jack in my life— no longer wants to see me because of a silly quarrel. He feels I chose my girls over him. I fear I've lost him forever.

It's been worse for my sister, though. Our private investigation team, Gladdy Gold and Associates, thought we were taking on a minor case at a posh retirement facility in Palm Beach, but it turned out to be dangerous for Evvie. She truly fell in love for the first time in her life, and it was almost the death of her. Evvie is overwrought with despair and can't face anyone; she's been hiding out, mostly in my apartment, ever since.

The doorbell rings. I don't need to guess who. It's the girls, ignoring our pathetic excuses and coming to drag us out of here. Evvie is rigid with fear. I kiss her cheek. "Just remember, all our neighbors think you're a hero, so get into your actress mode and convince them."

We are a rather ragtag group of seniors. We've all lived in Lanai Gardens in Fort Lauderdale for give or take twenty-five years. During those years we each had our own selection of friends. But as husbands and friends passed away, we regrouped. So now it's Evvie and me and three other women who take care of one another. Since I'm the only one still driving I seem to be the leader of this oddball pack of different personalities.

Our girls peer in through the screen door. Ida, arms folded, taps her foot impatiently. Sophie, grandly attired as usual in a color-coordinated bathing outfit from top to toes, has her hands on her hips. Bella meekly stands still, ever worried about making waves in our little private universe.

Here's a hair color update on our little gang. Ida, salt and pepper. Bella, totally white. Sophie, who changes color on a whim, flaunts her new shade of the month: apricot. Me, still lots of brown but getting grayer by the minute. However, Evvie's recently dyed vivid auburn hair shows no gray returning yet. I imagine every time she looks in the mirror she thinks of Philip, the man who made her feel young and beautiful again.

"So, *nu*," Ida says. "Coming or not coming?"

Evvie pushes open the screen, which makes them all jump out of her way. As she heads for the elevator she calls back at them, "Come on, let's get the show on the road."

The pool is The Pool. Attendance required. The gathering place of the residents of Lanai Gardens, Phase Two. Home of breaking news. Gossip hot off the griddle. Touch base time. With all the usual suspects. However, there are a few new permutations and combinations. Irving Weiss is not in attendance. Millie is now in a permanent Alzheimer's facility and he visits his beloved wife every single morning. Mary Mueller, our in-house nurse who saved Millie's life, drives him there every day.

Our newlyweds—Tessie Hoffman Spankowitz, an excitable fifty-six, and Sol Spankowitz, a decrepit and depressed seventy-nine—are in the pool. Hefty Tessie is trying to teach her new husband how to swim. It's hard to tell whether he is more terrified of drowning or of his wife.

Sol is not a happy man.

We all head for our usual chaise lounges.

Heaven forbid someone doesn't stick to the un-written seating chart. All hell would break loose.

"Hey, here they come," calls Hy Binder. "Just in time for my new joke."

One of the Canadians applauds Evvie. "Can't wait to hear about your big adventure."

No one is a fan of Hy's jokes. But then again, besides his brain-dead wife, Lola, who would be?

Evvie, who is wearing sunglasses and a huge straw hat to hide her face and feelings, parries back, "Hey, goody, goody, just in time." Needless to say, Evvie hates Hy's jokes but right now she'll stand for anything to keep herself out of the lime-light.

Hy jumps in fast before someone stops him. He bows to the newlyweds in the pool. "This joke is dedicated to the new Mr. and Mrs. Spankowitz."

Tessie grins and wraps her huge arms around Sol's puny, wattled, tense neck.

The Canadians make a point of going back to their newspapers and magazines. Many others groan. Evvie sits up to listen as if with rapt atten-tion.

Hy emotes. "Sam goes to his doctor and says, 'Doc, my wife is trying to poison me.' His doctor says, 'Sam, don't be silly.' He says, 'No, really, she's out to get me.' The doctor sighs and says, 'Bring your wife, Maisie, in to see me.' The next day he does and the doctor and Maisie go into his office. Sam waits outside. And waits and waits. Finally two hours later the doctor rushes out, his face a mass of sweat. 'What should I do, Doc?' Sam asks. 'Take the poison,' he says, 'take the poison!' "

Tessie looks confused. Sol nods, getting it.

Then the usual boos erupt, except for Sophie, who thinks it's hilarious and applauds.

Enya Slovak, our concentration camp survivor, looks up at him and says, "Hy Binder, shame on you!" With that, she goes back to reading her book.

Evvie abruptly stands. "I forgot I have to make an important call. Bye, gang." She walks away, leaving waves of disappointment. Our neighbors had hoped for some hot gossip.

Trying to cheer us up, Bella cooks dinner, her famous chicken soup with matzo balls, parsnips, and soup greens.

Bella's apartment is always immaculate. I don't know how she does it at eighty-three all by herself. The rest of us share a cleaning service that comes to help us out. Not Bella. She says she loves cleaning. And washing windows. And ironing. Yuk.

But tonight Bella's good intentions aren't working. I am not enjoying my dinner. Neither is Evvie, since the girls decided we needed a lecture along with our meal. The topic is their opinions about love. They each have a pet theme.

Ida, the man-hater: "Men are no good anyway. Who needs them?"

Sophie, Ms. Malaprop: "They're like buses. Another one will come along any year."

Bella: "I think men are nice. But I can't remember."

Now the advice gets specific. Aimed at me.

Evvie insists I call Jack. "You have the only good one; don't lose him." And then she bursts into tears.

Ida passes the tureen around. "I personally wouldn't shed a tear over a man."

Sophie helps herself to a third portion. "Go ahead, beg if you have to. You could always cross your fingers when you do it."

Bella daintily waves the soup away. "I like Jack. He's a mensch. So where did he say he was going? Miami Beach?"

I need to get the topic off me. "He didn't say. I've tried calling him, but he won't answer the phone. He doesn't want to talk to me. Look, I'm all right. It's Evvie who needs help."

She counters, "I don't need help. I just need some peace and quiet."

Ida: "Feeling sorry for yourself is stupid. Just hate him and be done with him."

Sophie: "I still can't get them straight. Who do you love? Philip or Ray?"

Bella: "What about the killer? He should get the chair!"

Evvie jumps up. "Everybody leave me alone!"

She hurries to the door. "Thanks for the soup. Next time, flank steak. My place." With that she's gone.

Bella is perturbed. "She didn't stay for the brownies."

2

FATHER AND SON NIGHT

"I should be getting home," Jack Langford says to his son, Morrie.

"It's only ten o'clock. What are you worried about? You'll turn into a pumpkin?"

"Very funny."

The two men are clearing the table in Morrie's small stucco house in the southern part of Fort Lauderdale. The kitchen and dining room form one unit, which makes it easy—perfect for a bachelor. "Too bad you're such a good cook," Jack comments, setting the plates in the sink.

"That's an odd thing to say, ungrateful even, since you polished off every bite of my beef Stroganoff."

"Maybe if you went hungry every night, you'd finally pick some nice girl and settle down."

"Now you sound like Mom." The men smile in memory of Faye, wonderful wife and mother.

"You're pushing forty, sonny boy."

"I might remind you, you didn't marry until you were forty."

Jack grins. He enjoys the teasing banter between the two of them. "That's different. In those lean days I needed to earn more money before I could settle down. And besides, we believed in long engagements." He reaches across the table for his wineglass and takes a sip.

"And what about Lisa?" Morrie rolls up his cuffs, turns on the hot water in the sink and squeezes soap on a sponge. "My sister didn't marry early, either. She wanted her career first. So, there you are; late marriage runs in the family."

Ignoring his futile argument, Jack plunges on, still smiling. "What was wrong with that beautiful redhead, Annie? I liked her."

"She was a micromanager and needed to know where I was every minute of the day. What I was thinking every moment. Not good for a cop's wife."

"And Lynn? You told me she was perfect."

"She was. For someone else. That's what she said when she returned my ring."

"Oops. You never told me that part."

"Hey, maybe I'm just unlucky in love."

"Or too picky. Keep looking. You better watch out or the guys in the station will think you're gay."

"Or smart. Especially the disillusioned, divorced ones."

It's a running joke between them, since Jack is a former cop himself, and Morrie's best friend—and former partner—Oz Washington, is gay. But everybody in the precinct knows Oz is a rotten cook. So much for stereotypes.

"You should talk." Morrie hands his dad a towel while he washes the plates. "What about Michelle? Why didn't you marry her? You were soooo in love. What was it, eight years ago when you took that trip to France?"

Jack is startled. He hasn't thought about her in a long time, having written off their month together as a brief fantasy. The beautiful, sexy Frenchwoman and the lonely American. The perfect vacation. The perfect love affair. Why had he been so afraid to bring her here? Wasn't he tempted to stay with her, to live in Paris? No, he couldn't be so far from his children. And he wasn't sure Michelle would have come to America; she was famous in Paris, with her own television talk show. And she was much younger. But Jack had never even asked her—he was so sure Michelle would turn him down.

"I'm sorry I ever mentioned it."

Morrie grins, mimicking, " 'Mentioned it?' You mooned around for months, drove us all crazy. 'Should I go back? Should I call?' "

"No use lamenting over something that's long

gone." Jack sighs. Fantasy, all fantasy. But every person should have one once in their lives.

"And now, Mr. Authority on Commitment, you haven't swept Gladdy Gold off her feet yet. I eagerly look at my mail every day waiting for my invitation to the wedding."

Jack shakes his head. "She hasn't emotionally buried her late husband yet. She thinks she has, but she hasn't. So she clings to her sister and her friends, afraid to move on."

"But she was willing to go away with you. To a secret island. Another perfect vacation?"

Jack swats his son with the damp towel. "It proves my point. If she really wanted to be alone with me, she wouldn't have told Bella where we were going. I suspect she was relieved to get the fax that forced us to come home early. On a subconscious level, that is."

"Thank you, Dr. Phil."

"She'd deny it, but I think I'm right."

By now all the dishes have been washed and dried. The two men head for the door.

"Eat and run, you're that kind of guy," says Morrie, punching his father gently on the shoulder.

"I guess I'm half hoping to get home and find a message from her on my machine."

"Hey, Dad, the phone works two ways. You could call her."

"No." Jack shakes his head. "She needs the time alone to work it out in her own mind."

"So your plan is to wait until she comes to you?"

"I'm working on a different plan. I'm thinking of going up to New York for a while."

"And . . . ?"

"Visit your sister and Dan and the kids."

"And? Stop stalling. I know you're up to something."

"Visit some of my old cronies in my old precinct . . ."

"And? More *and*s?"

"And try to reopen Gladdy's case and see if I can find the perp who murdered her husband."

Ignoring the amazement he knows will appear on Morrie's face, Jack opens the door and, not looking back, waves good night.

3

MORRIE DISSEMBLES

I've had it with my sister's problem.... Mine is different. No, let's be honest. Forget pride. I miss Jack terribly and I want answers. I need answers! If the father won't talk, I'll get it out of the son.

I keep leaving messages at the police station for Detective Morgan Langford but he never returns my calls. It must run in the family. Morrie knows perfectly well why I am calling. This time I don't request him, but ask the operator when he is expected in to work.

What a hypocrite I am, giving Evvie advice that I don't take for myself: Give up the impossible. I tell Evvie to walk away from Philip because it's a hopeless case, and here I am going behind her back to try and get Jack into my life again. Truly,

Evvie has no choice; she must find a way to go on without Philip. There is no chance they can ever be together again. So shouldn't I do the same with a man who no longer wants me? No! Not until I am very sure that's the case.

So here I am, waiting at the Lauderhill police station. It is fairly new and doesn't have the romance, if you will, of the old station, with its run-down seedy look and customers of the same persuasion. Where are the drooling drunks, the sarcastic punks, the fistfights? The awful smells of lives gone bad? Gone with the new architecture. This front waiting area is so clean and so dull, you would think you were at an accountant's office. I announce myself to the front window and I blatantly lie and tell them I have an appointment with Detective Morgan. Since I was told he was in, now let's see him get out of talking to me.

After a few moments during which I imagine he is wrestling with his conscience, Morrie finally comes out of the locked door. He is in his shirtsleeves and exudes an air of being busy.

I put my hands up. "I know. You don't have time. I only have one simple question: Where is your father?"

With that, he walks me outside, where I can face the new library, which shares the same parking area. I still prefer going to my old library, where I feel at home with old bookshelves and old friends. This new one is ultramodern, with a large room containing long banks of computers with kids playing games instead of doing their home-work; not for me.

"Look, Gladdy," Morrie says, "please don't put me in the middle."

"Why shouldn't I? You are in the middle. You know where he is and I want you to tell me."

I think I've surprised Morrie. He wouldn't ex-pect this frontal attack. He probably thinks I'd just wither away if he refused.

"I can't." Morrie holds firm.

"Because you don't know or he told you not to tell me?"

"Please let me go back inside and interrogate a man who might have just chopped up his wife with their garden ax. It would be easier than this."

"Coward."

"Yes. I am not at liberty to tell you anything and that's my final word."

"You sound like that old game show and I'm not promising you a million dollars. Okay." I change tactics. "Why doesn't Jack want me to know?"

"My lips are sealed."

"He's gone off with another woman?"

Morrie sputters at that. "He wouldn't—" Then stops.

I hide a tiny smile. That's a small victory, any-way. "Well, that's settled. Can you at least tell me when he'll be back?"

"I don't know."

Well, that's not a lie. I can see it in his eyes. He knows where he is, but he doesn't know when he'll be back.

"When you speak to him would you please give him a message?" I can feel my eyes tearing and my throat starting to choke up. "Please tell him I really need to talk to him."

Horribly uncomfortable, Morrie shrugs. Just before I turn away and head for my car, I toss this unkindness at him: "No wonder you're not married. You may not be scared of ax murderers, but you sure are scared of us women."

I don't really mean it, but I find satisfaction in rattling his cage. Somehow I feel better after this non-meeting. My Jack isn't off with another woman after all. He still loves me. I hope.

I can feel Morrie's eyes on my back as I reach my car.

As Ida once told me, sometimes a woman just has to be a bitch.

4

A NEW CASE

M eeting will come to order," announces Ida, tapping her teaspoon on her cup and opening her file folder.

With that, we all get ready for the weekly business meeting of Gladdy Gold and Associates. Our business slogan: "Senior sleuths for the senior citizen." Our motto: "Never trust anyone under seventy-five." Naturally all meetings include food. We're in Evvie's apartment; her turn to cook for the group meeting. I glance at her as she brings our lunch out from the kitchen. Her dark clothing lately is so unlike my Evvie, who always wore bright colors and wild patterns that expressed her usual upbeat demeanor.

And not that she's much of a hostess today, either. She's serving us takeout from the local deli, which she ordered and had delivered. Unheard of. We look forward to these meetings as an opportunity to share meals together and take turns showing off a little. Evvie's specialty is a superb chicken fricassee made with chicken wings and tiny meatballs. Her secret ingredient is Hungarian sweet paprika. But I digress.

Lately, Ida is the one keeping us all together.

While Sophie and Bella serve the coffee and strudel cake, Ida reviews a list of possible jobs. Actually, *a* job: Ida has culled the list down to the one she thinks will interest us. Evvie stays in the kitchen pretending to be very busy doing dishes. She promises to listen to us through the cutout pass-through. But we all know that she's avoiding dealing with reality and that all she wants to do is hide.

"We got a phone call from a Dr. and Mrs. Harvard Silverstone of Naples," Ida announces.

Bella, our secretary, takes out her notebook. "Where's that?" she asks.

"West coast Florida, directly across from us," Ida answers. "They are a couple in their nineties whose daughter lives in Fort Lauderdale. It seems that they have a very big anniversary coming up—number seventy-five—and they expect their daughter to attend."

Sophie is busily poking around the plate to find a piece of strudel that'll appeal to her. "So what's the big deal?"

"Yeah," echoes Bella, "where's the case?"

"Patience," Ida says. "Let me fill you in. Their only daughter, Linda, sends e-mail letters saying she can't come, but won't give a reason, other than to say she is too busy. When they call her they always get the answering machine. They haven't seen her in almost a year."

"That's not very nice of her," Bella comments.

"So what do they want of us?" Sophie asks.

I know I should contribute, but I can't get with it. I can see Evvie puttering about with her pots and pans and she looks so miserable. I wish I knew how to help her.

"Glad?" Ida says, trying to get my attention. "What do you think?"

"It doesn't seem too difficult. Visit the daughter and ask her straight out why she won't go. Why don't the three of you handle that?"

There's a silence as they absorb the fact that I am not including myself.

Sophie jumps in. "But you're our driver."

"I'm sure Denny will take you around." Our considerate handyman is always willing to help out the seniors who live in our Phase.

More silence. I know they are trying to figure out what to say.

Ida understands and is sympathetic, but her patience with our problems has its limits. She pushes back her chair. "Well, that takes care of that," she says curtly. "Come on, girls," she says to Sophie and Bella, "we have our assignment." Lots of ice in that tone, but frankly I don't blame her. Even I'm sick of my own self-pity.

Sophie looks longingly at the leftover strudel and grabs one for the road.

I shrug. "Sorry," I say.

"Thanks for lunch," says Bella, calling to Evvie in the kitchen on her way out, "but next time could we have the fricassee?"

Evvie mumbles something unintelligible.

The girls leave. I go into the tiny kitchen and sit down at the minuscule dinette table and chairs set. Evvie's back is to me.

"We've got to stop this, Ev."

Evvie turns. She's in tears. "I can't. I just can't. I'm so miserable." She drops down onto the other chair and leans her head on her arms. "I miss him every moment!"

With that she looks up at me pleadingly. "Maybe if I see him again one more time..."

I reach over and touch her arm. "Honey, you know you mustn't. It's over. You have to stop torturing yourself."

The doorbell rings.

"You answer," Evvie says. "Probably one of the girls left something. I don't want to talk to anybody."

To my immense surprise there is a familiar man standing on the other side of the screen door: Joe Markowitz, Evvie's ex-husband. I haven't seen him in years. I can't help but stare. Time hasn't been good to him. He seems to have shrunk from his original five foot seven. His back has rounded out like a man with osteoporosis. There's not much left of his original curly black hair, only shreds of gray tufts. His black eyes, which once seemed big and glittering, are pale and washed out. The expression on his face is mournful.

He manages a small smile. "Hello, Gladdy. Long time no see."

I can't take my eyes off him. "Evvie, come look who's here."

Evvie comes to the door. Her eyes widen in shock. "Joe? What the hell are you doing here?"

He gives her a half-toothless grin. "Guess what. I've just moved down to Florida. And guess what. I rented an apartment right here in Lanai Gardens."

For a moment, she is speechless. Then, "Oh, swell," she says in disgust, "just what I needed."

5

BREAKFAST WITH
THE BICKERSONS

We're sitting at my dining room table—Evvie, Joe, and I—sipping coffee.

There used to be a radio show my mother and I listened to when I was growing up. Way before there was television. It was hilarious. It was about a couple named Bickerson, John and Blanche, who did nothing but bicker. (Get it? Bickering Bickersons? Shows were kind of simplistic those days.) Don Ameche and Frances Langford, two wonderful actors, played the parts. But they had nothing on the couple airing their show in my apartment this morning. The bickering Markowitzes.

Yesterday Joe stayed only a few moments to give Evvie news she didn't want. The way she put it, after he left, was that she'd rather have the heartbreak of psoriasis. But I immediately had it in my head that maybe Joe might take her mind off Philip, so I invited them both for breakfast. I guess it's working, though perhaps not in the way I imagined.

Evvie says, "So in all of Fort Lauderdale, you had to pick this place to plant your *tuckus*?"

Joe says, "I thought it would be nice to be near family." With this he looks pleadingly at me.

I shrug. "Sure, that's a good reason. More coffee?"

Evvie: "No." She glares at me. Translation: Why did she ever let me talk her into this stupid breakfast?

Joe: "Sure, thanks, you always did make a good cup of java, Glad."

I, however, remember a different Joe, criticizing everything anyone in our family did. My coffee he called "like mud." Seems like Joe is rewriting history. In the past he never wanted to have anything to do with us.

Evvie, helping herself to more pancakes: "So our daughter finally got sick of having to take care of you? She threw you out?"

Joe: "Martha did no such thing. She liked having me live with them."

Evvie: "I'll bet. But then again, I remember she always used to take in ugly stray dogs. Out of pity."

Joe, getting hot under the collar: "I was a big

help to them. Her Elliot couldn't change a light-bulb without me."

Evvie: "Yeah, yeah. I remember how good you were around our apartment. I had to get on my hands and knees and beg before you'd ever change a lightbulb for me."

"More syrup?" I ask, putting my body between theirs before they come to blows. Both of them push the bottle away, narrowly missing spilling that sticky stuff on me. I'd better not get too close.

Evvie daintily wipes her mouth. "I always meant to ask how come your darling family didn't take you in when you went broke? Again."

Joe, hotter: "My sisters wanted to. Only they had their own kids living with them!"

Evvie, under her breath: "Losers, one and all."

Joe stands. He never could take anything bad said against his clan. "I heard that. Take it back!"

Evvie, standing also: "Why should I? Truth is truth. And besides I'm not married to you any-more, so I don't have to pretend to like people who hate me!"

Joe, moving swiftly to the door, his napkin still under his chin: "And vice-a-versa, babe. Vice-a-versa!"

One slam of the front door screen, then an-other.

Evvie's voice outside my kitchen window. "Go downstairs the other way. I can't stand the sight of you!"

"Vice-a-versa again, bitch!"

Silence. That went well, I think, smiling. Then my smile fades as I remember Joe when we first met. Standing tall, wearing his army uniform proudly. It was late 1944; the war was soon to come to its dramatic end, but we didn't know that yet. Excitement was in the air. Danger. Couples falling in love and marrying just before the men were shipped out overseas. The women not knowing whether their husbands would ever return. Evvie and Joe were caught up in the drama. With his curly black hair and flashing dark eyes, Joe was a looker! And Evvie, the exciting, beautiful redhead, so in love. The two of them holding hands and looking at one another, their shining glances saying This is it. This is real love and it will last forever.

Joe came back alive and then reality set in.

I can still hear them shouting at one another from the stairwells.

Oh, well, at least it took her mind off Philip.

6

NEW YEAR'S EVE 1961

THE SCREAM

A woman screamed. For a moment, everything and everyone seemed to freeze. The street was still. The air seemed not to move. Then, almost in slow motion, Gladdy saw Jack turn toward the alley from where that chilling sound came. And, without thought, he started running toward it. Gladdy felt herself reacting too slowly. By the time she found her voice and called after him, "Jack, no!" he was already out of sight.

A heart-stopping moment later she heard her husband shout, "Patty, run!"

And then the shot.

To her ears it was as if a small firecracker went off, but she knew in her heart this was something worse. She'd never before heard gunfire, but she understood that's what it was. In the same almost *paralyzed moment she and Emily looked fearfully at one another. Then again out the window at the alley. Surely Jack would reappear and grin up at them and tell them it was some false alarm.*

Why fool herself? This was something bad. Gladdy ran for the door, not even taking her coat. With a last anguished look at her daughter, she raced out.

"Stay here, Emily!" she cried as the door slammed behind her.

7

NEW YORK JACK

When Jack climbs out of the taxi in front of his hotel, he stops to smell the air. Nowhere in the world smells like New York. He is instantly jazzed. The city does that to him. He smiles as he watches the mobs of people moving along the street. Just about every single one of them has a cell phone to an ear.

He's purposely chosen this hotel because it's closest to his former precinct. It looks kind of run-down, but it works with his budget. He thinks ruefully that his cop's pension was small when he retired years ago, but now it's ridiculous in these inflated times. There is no room for grandiose expenditures. A thought pushes into his head about the money it cost to take Gladdy on that impromptu runaway trip to Pago Pago. Be a

long time until that credit card is paid off. Well—
he smiles remorsefully—it was almost worth-
while.

He has called his old buddy Tim Reilly in advance, and Tim is waiting for him at his old
precinct. At least he knows one guy who is still
there.

After checking in, Jack drops his bags in his
room and walks out again. He doesn't want to
take a cab or bus; he just wants to walk the city
streets and absorb every image. The cop in him
comes back instantly and he finds his eyes darting
all over, taking everything in. His back straightens, his step quickens. He is home.

How he's longed for this city. It crept into your
bones, and no matter how far you went, or for
how long, you never forgot it; you never stopped
missing your true emotional home. How many
times over these years since Faye died has he con-
templated moving back? New York is alive, while
Florida—let's face it; they call it God's waiting
room to wherever the hell or heaven you go to
next.

But he stays in Fort Lauderdale because of
Morrie. Because Morrie became a cop, too, and
Jack wants to remain close. To advise and just
be there for him. Then again, had he left, he
wouldn't have met Gladdy Gold. *B'shert*. Fate.

Anyway, it's been a while since he's visited his
daughter, Lisa, and Dan and the boys. About time
he came to see his latest grandchild.

He knows, before he eventually heads back to Florida, he has to make one other stop: Zabar's. The ultimate take-out deli. The best in the whole world.

Funny, he reflects, Gladdy and her husband, Jack, had lived on the West Side, too. Faye and I probably hit Zabar's to shop at the same time they did on some Sunday mornings. I must ask Gladdy about that.

Walking into that store with its thousand luscious smells. Picking up bagels, lox, whitefish, and cream cheese for the ritual Sunday morning family breakfast. Oh, yes, and the heft of the hernia-causing *New York Times*. What great memories.

He smiles as he passes an alley. Not such great smells in there.

He even likes the noise of the garbage trucks picking up in the middle of the night. Oh, well, he thinks happily, once a New Yorker, always a New Yorker.

Same old precinct on Fifty-fourth Street. Jack walks inside. Doesn't look as ratty as it used to. Still smells just as bad from years and years of piss and vomit and worse; and above all, fear. He is amused at himself, at how he is so aware of the odors in the city in contrast to Florida. People waiting in the police station look the same as always, bedraggled, aggressive, and frightened. He wonders if the plumbing is the same. The pipes used to roar every time someone used the johns.

Jack gives his name to the desk sergeant as he glances at the cop on duty. God, he thinks, was I ever that young?

He is directed to Detective Timothy Reilly's office. Reilly stands up as he enters, then hurries to him. They bear-hug. Tim is as genuinely glad to see him as he is to see Tim. They look one another over. Tim hasn't changed all that much. Just everything rounder and heavier. Still the same cowlick popped up on top of that Irish carrot-red head now sprinkled with gray. Jack wonders how he shapes up compared to his old buddy.

"How come they haven't sent you out to pasture yet?" Jack asks.

Tim laughs. "I'm the only one left who knows where the bodies are buried." Tim pours himself a refill from a thermos. "Green tea?" he offers as they sit down.

A raised eyebrow is Jack's response. "What? No more station-house sludge for coffee?"

Tim points to his chest. "The old ticker can't handle that slop anymore. The wife read some article about Japanese green tea keeping you alive longer."

Jack holds up his cup. "As I recall, Mary Lou was never wrong about anything." He grins.

"You got that right." Tim grins, too.

Jack runs through a litany of names. Wondering where all the old gang are. "Morton?"

"Dead. Heart attack."

"Janowsky?"

"Retired. Mexico."

"Porter?"

"Dead. Died in his bed."

"Furino?"

"Shot in a domestic three years ago, had to re-tire."

Jack apologizes for not staying in touch. "I promised," he says contritely.

"That's what they all say," Tim answers. "Nobody does. Once they're out of here... fugeddaboudit. How's the kid? He always wanted to be a cop like Daddy. End up as a fireman?"

"Morrie stayed the course. He's a detective in my own local precinct, not five minutes from where I live in Fort Lauderdale."

"Way to go. My boy grew up to be a Con Edison repairman. He always did hate the sight of blood."

"And Mary Lou?"

"Same old, same old. Really old," Tim says, grinning. "She won't let me retire. No way I come home and sit around and mess up her house. Her house." This is an old joke and they laugh at it. All the guys used to say they were more afraid of retirement than any perp, because their wives would murder them for being underfoot.

"So what's this about? You didn't come to see if I got uglier than you."

Jack takes a deep breath. "I want to open an old case. A cold case."

Tim grimaces. "Too much sunburn? Or maybe those TV shows they got now made you homesick."

"I met a woman."

"Ahh. You old dog, you."

"Her husband was murdered. Twenty-sixth precinct. New Year's Eve, 1961. Someone attacked a girl. Her husband played hero and got a bullet in the gut. College professor. Columbia."

Tim looks at him incredulously. "Getoutta here! A case over forty years ago? You gotta be kidding."

"It's standing in the way of her committing to marry me."

Tim smiles wryly. "Come on. That's crazy. Tell her to snap out of it."

"I wish it were that easy."

"And you want to solve it now? You? Single-handed? I don't have to tell you how idiotic you sound."

"Don't I know it?"

Tim Reilly sits back in his swivel chair, examining his old buddy's determined face. He shakes his head unbelievingly. "You remember that old TV show? Must have been way back in the fifties— 'There's a million stories in the naked city'? That's it, *Naked City*. And you have to pick the one in a million impossible ones."

Jack looks sheepishly at him. "Guess so."

"You really intend to go through with this? I can't talk you out of it."

" 'Fraid not."

"I hope you didn't promise your lady love that you'd solve it, O hero cop?"

"She doesn't even know I'm here."

"Good, keep it that way. 'Cause when you fall on your ass she won't know that, either."

Jack grins. "You will help me, won't you?"

"Couldn't think of any other sucker?"

" 'Fraid you're it."

"You know it ain't gonna be easy."

"That's why I came to you. So you'll give the guys at the Twenty-sixth a heads-up?"

"Wouldn't miss their catcalls for anything." Tim stands and pretends to swat him with a folder. "Like there's anybody else dumb enough around here *but* me." Jack pretends to duck. "You're gonna make me go out on a limb for you and you not even sending me a damn postcard with some orange trees all these years?"

They both laugh. Jack places his hand over his heart. "Mea culpa."

"Yeah. Like you know from mea culpa."

Tim walks Jack to the door. "Don't call me, I'll call you. What fleabag are you staying in?"

Jack shakes Tim's hand. "The Dartford down the corner. And I'm itching already. Thanks for the support."

"*De nada.*" Tim grins. "You always were a sucker for lost causes."

Jack starts to walk down the hall. Tim calls after him. "How long are ya staying in town? Have time for a Yankees game?"

"Sure," he says. "Depends on you. If I get this thing solved real fast, you're on."

"Then, that's a no, I take it."

Jack grins, feeling wonderful. Nothing like old friends. He's glad he found Tim again.

8

JACK'S FAMILY

Jack sits on a bench in the neighborhood pocket park across the street from where his daughter, Lisa, lives on New York City's West Side. It's a wonderful spot with a perfect view of the Hudson River. Only a few minutes ago a ship—he was sure it was a British ocean liner—passed them heading for its pier.

He gazes happily at his three adorable grandchildren: the two older boys, Jeremy, eleven, and Jeffrey, thirteen, and three-month-old Molly, asleep in her carriage. The boys, who look like towheaded athletic twins, are on the grass playing with their brand-new Game Boys. Jack is exhausted. One trip to the FAO Schwarz toy store and he's running on empty, as is his wallet. He's glad to be sitting down.

Lisa, right next to him, lifts her face up to the sun. "Are you sure you won't stay with us, Dad? We can take Molly into our room; it's no big deal."

"And keep you and Dan up all night?" Jack shook his head. "I'm better off in the hotel down where I am. It's more convenient to—" He breaks off.

"Does it have to do with why you're here?"

The autumn leaves are falling around them and Jack recalls how he used to take the whole family on yearly trips up to New England when the leaves turned color. It was almost a New York ritual.

"What are you thinking?" Lisa asks.

"I was remembering the fall trips we took to see the leaves. Your mother always looked forward to them."

"Me, too. I used to love going to the bed-and-breakfasts where they had those fluffy down featherbeds and all the antiques and such fancy food for breakfast. It seemed like we were in a different century. Morrie never wanted to go. He wanted to stay home with his pals because it was the beginning of football season. We had to drag him along. Remember?"

Jack nods. "No matter how long I live down in Florida, I still miss the change of seasons."

"I know. But surely you don't miss the ice and snow?" Lisa takes a good look at her father. "So, why are you really here, Dad? This isn't your usual once-a-year jaunt." She tosses her hair.

She looks so much like Faye did at her age, he thinks, so beautiful. Same curly blond hair. He remembered how Faye tried so hard to keep her unruly locks in place; today's women let them fly wildly. Lisa had her mother's bright, inquisitive green eyes, too, and the same lithe body.

"I came to see my new grandchild."

She tosses him a knowing look. "Come on, Dad."

He hesitates. "It's complicated."

"We've got nothing else to do. The roast is in the oven. Dan won't be home for an hour. If I take the boys up now they'll run around to let off steam and drive us crazy—better to stay outdoors. So talk."

"There's a woman..."

She grins. "I know. You think my brother doesn't report to me? Have you a happy announcement to make? Did you come here to get my blessing?"

"You mean you're not upset? It's not like I'm replacing your mother."

Lisa snuggles up to him, playfully rubbing her arm along his. "You're still here, Dad; you're lucky to find love again."

"Her name is Gladys Gold. Gladdy. She lives in Phase Two."

"So Morrie says. That's convenient. You don't even have to drive." Lisa smiles.

"She's not quite sure she wants to marry again."

Lisa leans her shoulder on Jack for a moment. "She must be playing hard to get. What woman could resist you?"

"This one. Thanks. Flattery will get you everywhere."

"So what's the problem? Cold feet? I can understand that. At your age change must be difficult."

He pretends to look angry. "What about my age...?"

She punches his shoulder, smiling. The boys run off to play catch with their new baseball gloves. Lisa adjusts her view so she can keep an eye on them.

"Her husband was murdered. A long time ago."

She turns again, swiftly, shocked. "No!"

"Yes. Not far from here. Right near Columbia. He taught there, and on a New Year's Eve he was shot saving a girl's life. Never found the killer."

"How terrible. That's a trauma that you never get over."

"Precisely. Perhaps if there was closure for her... I'm here to reopen the case."

He sees how surprised Lisa is. This is a startling piece of information to have thrown at her cold, like this. After she ponders it for a few moments she looks up at him thoughtfully. "Dad," she says softly. "Still tilting at windmills?"

"I doubt I'll get anywhere, but I feel I have to try." Lisa places his hand in hers. They sit like that, quietly, lost in their own thoughts, as the boys play and the baby sleeps.

9

CONDO DOINGS

We are in the rec room for our monthly Lanai Gardens Phase Two business meeting where one and all gather to complain about plumbing problems, roof leaks, whatever, so that our condo association might do something about it. Or not. Mostly it is a time to get together and shmooze and exchange gossip.

We have the meeting at three P.M., the so-called cocktail hour. So-called because only soft drinks are allowed. This was decided years ago by the board, for two reasons: one, no more getting snockered with resulting harsh words said that could never be taken back, and two, so the meeting will be short. Nobody wants to miss the early-bird dinners around town. But there are plenty of things to nosh on to get them through—a dollop of smoked salmon, a smidgen of chopped liver, Chinese egg rolls. Empty stomachs make for grumbling; full ones can suffer a little longer with whatever grievances they have. These treats are contributed by the refreshment committee, which seems to have an unlimited budget. Sometimes I think we get such a big draw for the hors d'oeuvres only.

Usually, as Phase Two secretary, Evvie runs the meeting, but Ida is taking over for her today. Everybody is aware that Evvie is suffering over a lost love affair. But nobody dares ask questions. Evvie won't allow it. Which gives the gossipmongers plenty of room to speculate. Meanwhile, my sister is sitting in the very last row in the back and I keep her company.

Denny Ryan sits in the front row, wielding his notepad. He is our fixer-upper janitor and awaits job orders. Yolie, Millie's caregiver, is at his side as always. Now that Millie is in the Alzheimer's hospital, Yolie only takes care of Irving. The rest of the time she's with her boyfriend, Denny.

Irving arrives just then. He's with Mary, who just brought him back from the hospital. They take seats together in one of the rows.

Needless to say, newlywed Tessie is there showing off her husband, Sol. She is seen everywhere with him these days. In Publix Market, she walks proudly behind as he pushes the shopping cart. At the beauty shop Sol is dutifully seated, waiting for his wife to get prettied up—not an easy task, that.

They're at the bank, her arm holding his tightly. And just as tightly, holding his bank account book. Tessie is making sure the universe knows she finally nabbed a man, even though he's as old as dirt. Is that what's putting the rosy cheeks on her these days?

The young cousins, Barbi and Casey—who have been very helpful to us with their business, a computer research service they call Gossip—attend dutifully, but they don't speak up. Sometimes I think they watch us old folks like anthropologists doing research on a strange and bizarre species.

I notice Joe Markowitz has turned up, even though he's not in our Phase. He keeps trying to get Evvie's attention, but she ignores him. Is this a new Joe—a glutton for punishment?

The remaining few men of our condo are off to one side, shooting pool, their macho way of showing uninterest in anything women will run. The clicking of the balls emphasizes their arrogance. Anything to be annoying. Hy, the ringleader, tries to smack the balls the hardest. Naturally Lola is standing nearby, waiting with the little cube of chalk, telling him what a wonderful player he is.

Voices drone on. I find myself drifting off, glancing at the walls filled with photos celebrating the last twenty-five years or so of Phase Two activities. I spot a picture of a New Year's Eve event about fifteen years ago. I'm in it along with

Evvie and Sophie and Bella; Francie, may she rest in peace; Millie, now as good as gone forever; and others, also gone. I sigh. I know. I know how old I am. But still, it seems like time has moved too fast.

At that moment, Sophie and Bella hurry to my side.

"We gotta talk," Sophie says with urgency. "As soon as this is over." The girls sit down alongside Evvie and me.

Ida finishes reading the minutes of the last meeting. And announces some upcoming events such as the big Halloween bash next month. Everyone enjoys dressing up and allowing their inner child to play. She looks up. "Any new business?"

Ruth Novak's hand shoots up. She's in S311. "I have a question for the medications committee." She is a sweet, quiet lady and she says fearfully, "Every day I put out my medications and I get so confused sometimes which day it is and I forget which pills I already took...." She stops, showing the confusion she feels.

Mary, head of the committee, stands up. "We suggest you buy those one-week traveling plastic pill containers, maybe get two or three for that many weeks. Then sit down when you feel clear in your mind, or call one of us on the committee and we'll do it with you, and fill all of them up at one time. That way, we'll also figure out when you need to reorder, so you won't feel muddled every day."

There is a smattering of applause, but I hear from the whispers in the row in front of me that the gossip has already started. How come Mary drives Irving to the hospital all the time? How come as soon as Millie is not around, Irving is already with another woman? No, no, Irving, he's a saint. What's the matter with you? Mary's a nurse. She's taking care of him. Yeah, maybe too much care. Remember her husband dumped her—the speaker's voice drops—for another man? She's still a young woman with needs—wink, wink.

Another hand is raised. Sandy Sechrest, a schoolteacher from R115, says, "I just read an article that said that a car company can move its factories to Mexico and claim it's a free market. A bank can incorporate in Bermuda and claim it's a free market. We buy massive amounts of American products made in China, India, and a very large number of different countries, all considered free markets. Then how come senior citizens who dare buy their prescription drugs from a Canadian pharmacy are called un-American!"

Len Riegert, one of the pool players, waves his cue stick up in the air. "Right on, Sandy!"

Others mumble to themselves in agreement. Some call out. It's a hot issue.

"Write to AARP."

"Call our congressmen."

"Down with the drug company lobbyists!"

Ida knocks on her table with her fist. "Okay, everybody calm down. Maybe it's time we started a political action committee."

Hands shoot up at that. Len, still excited, says, "I'll start it. Sandy, you join us. Anyone else interested, meet me after the meeting. Just remember, folks, seniors are now getting to be nearly forty-eight percent of the population. Our votes count!"

Sophie can't resist asking, "So how come if we're almost half of all the people in America, the TV shows are only about young people? A lot of dumb young people!"

Cheers for Sophie. "You tell 'em Soph," someone in the back yells.

"Dump the TV," says another. "Go back to reading books."

Hy is annoyed. "Enough with the politics," he says to Len. "Let's get back to the game."

Another hand frantically goes up. Polly Hessel from apartment Q411, dressed as usual in tank top, shorts, and sweatband, no matter the weather, stands up and faces the group. "I saw a spider in my apartment."

This brings on worried groans. Can roaches be far behind? If there is one topic that unites them all, it's the terror of infestation.

"Was it big?" Pat Steiner from T116 asks breathlessly.

"Big, very big. And hairy."

A shiver of fear can be felt round the room.

Hy calls out, "Stop talking about my private parts." He laughs raucously.

He gets his usual response—a lot of boos, and someone throws peanuts at him. The other men laugh to show solidarity for their comrade.

The women go back to the business at hand. "Did you see any more of them?" Vicki Goff from R414 asks.

"No," says Polly, "just one, but maybe Denny can come up and look around. And maybe spray a little bit."

Denny nods and makes a notation in his notepad.

"So what did you do?" Margaret Ramona, one of the Canadian renters, asks. Heavy drama is building up here.

"First I climbed on the sofa." Polly pauses for dramatic effect.

"Then?" the women ask in unison. Eyes are big and round and captivated.

"Then I said, Who's afraid of an itty-bitty spider?"

"I thought you said it was big," Pat, a stickler for accuracy, accuses.

"And hairy," dittos Vicki.

Polly ignores the question. "I took my can of Mace and blasted him to hell!"

Lots of oohs and ahhs at that.

"Where did you get Mace?" Lola calls from next to Hy.

"My wonderful son got it for me to keep me out of danger."

"What danger? You never go out anywhere." Ida can't resist. This woman is taking up all their time.

"I might. Someday."

Hy, pulling Lola, starts for the door. He's had it. "Enough about bugs. If there's nothing more important, can we get out of here?"

That's all it takes. One person heading out for dinner—can the others be far behind? The exodus begins. Leon Uris, where are you when we need you?

But that doesn't stop a number of them from cornering Denny with their apartment complaints. They set up appointments with him.

Ida shrugs, and then calls the meeting to an end. She joins us at the back as the room empties out.

"Now?" asks Sophie.

"Go ahead. Tell them," Ida says.

Bella looks forlorn. "We already failed on our new case."

Sophie agrees. "We called and called Dr. Silverstone's daughter, Linda, so we could tell her how much her parents wanted her to come visit, and all we ever get is the machine."

Ida continues. "We even got Denny to drive us to her house, but it's a great big place behind a huge gate. We didn't dare ring the bell."

"We wanted to look in the windows but there

was no way, and from a distance it looked like all the drapes were drawn," says Sophie.

"But we think we could hear music or the TV playing," Bella adds.

This surprises me. "But she has to go out sometime. Did you hang around awhile?"

"We only stayed about an hour. Denny had to get back to unclog a toilet in the Rose building. Nothing."

They look to me for guidance. I guess I have to get involved. "All right, time for a longer stakeout. Don't you agree, Ev?"

But Evvie ignores my pathetic attempt to engage her. She sees Joe bearing down on her and quickly rises. "I have a headache. I'm going home." With that she leaves us.

Joe sees the rebuff, and does a hard about-face.

Sophie jumps ahead. "There's a nice mall real close to where Linda Silverstone lives. We could take turns sitting in the car while the rest of us shop. Or take turns having lunch at the deli."

Ida shakes her head. "A two-track mind, as usual. Shopping and food."

Bella applauds Sophie. "A great plan."

Yeah, great, I think.

Bella tugs at Sophie. "Come on, we're late. It's bingo and pizza night at Phase Five. Ida, you coming? Glad?"

"Why not?" Ida says. I shake my head no.

The girls take off. I realize I'm the only one left in the rec room. I shut the lights, close the door, and make my way down the bridge path toward my apartment.

There is a sound somewhere off to one side of the bridge. Then I see them, standing half hidden by a palm tree. Irving and Mary are whispering. A moment later they lean toward one another, kissing gently.

Oh, my, I think. This will cause an uproar around here; sparks will fly. They look so sweet together. Poor Irving. Millie's been sick so long. He deserves a little happiness. And so does Mary for that matter.

I think sadly, Don't I deserve a little happiness, too?

10

COLD CASE

As Jack, holding his cell phone, walks to the window of his small, generic hotel room, he assesses its few amenities: an ancient TV that's bolted to the wall, ditto the tarnished mirror. A rickety lamp with a lightbulb so low, it's impossible to read at night. Glancing into the bathroom, he notes the one threadbare towel and one washcloth. Good thing he doesn't intend to bring anyone to this pathetic excuse for a hotel accommodation. He looks down below.

"Yeah," he says on his cell phone to Morrie. "Got a great view of an air shaft, and the noise of the air conditioner unit down below could deafen a person."

"Why don't you go somewhere else?" Morrie comments.

Behind Jack, spread out on his bed, are dozens of folders. They look as old and faded as the shabby bedspread. "As long as it's clean, it suits my purpose."

He pictures his son leaning back in his office chair, with his feet propped up on his desk, prepared to listen to his dad's adventures in the Big Apple. "And here I was expecting you to be getting ready for a night on the town."

"Dinner at your sister's was excitement enough. By the way, the boys said to say hello to Uncle Morrie and not to forget their birthdays are coming up. And your sister and brother-in-law send regards, too."

"Thanks. Bet those kids wore you out."

"Never, never take eleven- and thirteen-year-olds to FAO Schwarz unless you've gone into heavy training in advance. Frankly, I hate to admit it, I'm glad to be staying in this dump for the peace and quiet."

Jack walks back to the bed, moves papers around to make room for himself, and stretches out. He occasionally glances over at the files next to him.

"Any luck on the case?" Morrie asks.

"Tim Reilly is fantastic. I guess he called in a lot of markers for this information. I pulled everything I could out of the old files, but it's one of those no-win situations. Nobody saw anything or heard anything. The guys canvassed the entire neighborhood." Jack tries to downplay his frustration. He props the pillows behind his head, trying to get comfortable.

"What about the girl? His student. What did she say about the attack? How did she come to be in the alley? Did she recognize the guy?"

The pillows are too large and stiff. He pushes them off to one side and gets up.

"Apparently Patty Dennison was a fragile young woman who went to pieces because her favorite teacher died saving her. She was hospitalized, severely traumatized. Couldn't speak. Couldn't remember anything. Her family took her out of school and left the city. Never came back."

"Pretty much a dead end?"

"Looks like it."

"What's your next step?"

"I was thinking about going to see Gladdy's daughter, Emily. She was only eleven at the time. Ironic, she has a daughter that same age now. And the same age as our Jeremy. In fact, Lisa found out the two kids go to the same school and are in the same class."

"Hey, what a coincidence." He pauses. "Pretty awful, Dad, to think of a kid that age going through what Gladdy's little girl did."

As Jack paces his small room, he stops to pick up a dropped piece of paper and adds it to the pile on his bed.

Morrie goes on. "Interesting dilemma you have

there. Wanting to visit the daughter of the lady you hope to marry without said lady even knowing about your intentions."

"It will be quite a surprise for Emily. I have no idea what Glad's told her about me. If anything. In fact, get this: Lisa is taking me to Welcome Back to School Night. Kind of a transition event to take the kids from summer fun to schoolwork again. Maybe I'll get a chance to meet Emily there. Funny, our daughters live only a few blocks from one another."

"And if you meet her in Jeremy's classroom, what will you do?" Morrie sounds curious.

"I'll ask her if she'll speak to me. If not, then I won't bother her."

"Why don't you call her first and warn her?"

"I think I need to surprise her and catch her off guard. I don't want her too comfortable."

"Once a cop, always a cop." Morrie's tone is amused.

"By the way, have you seen or heard anything about Gladdy lately?" Jack asks carefully. He misses her greatly and can't admit it to his son.

"She has a new case. The Lanai Gardens grapevine's still going strong." He stops and Jack realizes he's being punished by his son.

"What's it about?" He laughs, trying to get Morrie to say more. "Come on, you can tell me."

"No, and if you want to find out more, the ball is in your court. She specifically asked me to tell you to call."

Jack is surprised. "You spoke to her?"

"She actually came down to the station and trapped me in a corner."

Jack smiles. That's his Gladdy, all right. "How did she sound?"

"Pretty mad, I think. I don't like being put in the middle." He tries to sound grumpy, but Jack can hear the caring in his voice.

"Stop nagging," Jack says gruffly. "I'll call when I'm ready."

"Yes, sir. If you could see me, I'm saluting."

Guilt, guilt, guilt, Jack thinks. He should have confided in Gladdy. But he was afraid of raising her hopes or, worse, being told to leave the case alone. How will he ever make it up to her?

11

OPEN HOUSE

As Jack enters Middle School 44, with eleven-year-old Jeremy hanging on one arm and thirteen-year-old Jeffrey on the other, he is reminded of the times he accompanied Lisa and Morrie in their early days of elementary school so many years ago. Talk about déjà vu. It is the winters he remembers the most, for he always had to help the kids with their heavy coats and galoshes before they went running off to their classes.

Lisa is right behind them. Dan has stayed home to take care of the baby.

All school buildings seem to smell the same. Chalk dust and regular dust and old gym shoes. It feels wonderfully alive. The boys, like energetic young colts, drag him along at as fast a pace as they can get him to move.

Lisa laughs. "You're always this excited when school starts. Three days later, what will you kids say?"

The boys answer together: "I'm bored!"

"Exactly."

The walls are filled with some of last year's best artwork and science posters. Jack shows suitable appreciation as the boys make Jack look at every single one until they find Jeremy's. It is a picture of a boy riding a horse in a park. Jeremy explains, grinning through his braces, that it's him riding in Central Park.

"Enough dawdling," Lisa says. "We'll be late."

They climb up to the second floor. Tonight it's Jeremy's sixth-grade class. Tomorrow they'll meet Jeffrey's teachers.

The room is already crowded. The youngish, athletic-looking teacher, Mr. Fieldstone, seems to be very popular as the boys and girls crowd round, eager to introduce their parents. Jeremy pulls loose to grab on to his buddies with a lot of back-slapping and high-fiving. As if they hadn't seen one another almost every day of the summer.

Jack glances at the mothers, wondering how he'll recognize Emily if she's here. He's seen photos of her in Gladdy's apartment, but that might not be enough. He and Lisa watch as Jeremy slowly approaches a girl, who smiles shyly at him. He smiles shyly back, and suddenly, with a silly grin forming on his face, he attempts to smooth back his unruly mop of blond hair.

"Oh, my," Lisa says, grinning. "That must be the Lindsay who Jeffrey keeps teasing him about." The girl is adorable, standing there with her wide mischievous eyes and reddish-brown pigtails and dimples. And she has braces also. She is giggling, putting her hands over her mouth. It's obvious how much she likes her nervous suitor.

But it's her mother standing next to her who Jack finds himself staring at. He knows at once it has to be Emily. He sees Gladdy in her lovely oval-shaped face and in her relaxed posture. And her smile, he'd know that smile anywhere. And the simple pleated dress she's wearing—Gladdy's preferred beiges and browns.

Jeremy turns redder and redder and seemingly becomes totally tongue-tied.

Jeffrey is about to go over and make his brother even more miserable, but Lisa grabs his shirt and holds him back. "Don't even think about it."

Emily is standing next to a man—her husband, Alan, Jack assumes—and another of their children, a boy, about fifteen. That would be Patrick. For a moment he watches their animated chatting. Emily and Alan are both dark-haired and tall. He remembers Gladdy telling him that Alan is a doctor, a pediatrician. He has a kind face and Jack assumes his small patients feel comfortable with him. He likes the way Alan holds his wife's hand.

"It's Emily," Jack tells Lisa. "I recognize her."

"And Lindsay's her daughter?" Lisa grins. "We may someday have two matches from the Gold family."

Jack grins and pokes her playfully.

Lisa glances at Jack. "Ready to make your move?" By now it's almost her turn to greet Jeremy's teacher and she gives Jack a little push before she moves up in the line.

Jack strolls over to where Jeremy is listening avidly to what Lindsay is saying about the ballet classes she's taking this year. Jeremy breathes a sigh of relief at being rescued from his inability to mumble a word on such an alien subject. "Hi, Grandpa."

"Would you introduce me to your friend?"

He's able to do that. "This is Lindsay and that's her mom and dad and brother." It all comes rushing out of his mouth as if it were one run-on word. With that, Lindsay says hi and pulls Jeremy away with her as she spots other friends.

Jack introduces himself. "Jack Langford."

Alan says, "We're the Levinsons; Emily, Alan, and Patrick. And of course, Lindsay, who's run off with your grandson. Not literally, of course."

"Your name is familiar," Emily comments, squinting at him.

"I hoped it would be. I come from Fort Lauderdale."

Her eyebrows lift and she grins. "Lanai Gardens? That Jack?"

"Gladdy's Jack?" Alan adds, equally surprised.

There's a lot of smiling and shaking hands. Jack points to Lisa, who's been watching. She waves. "That's my daughter, Lisa, and my other grandson, Jeffrey."

Alan says, "Well, how about that? We all live in the same neighborhood."

Emily is beaming. She teases him. "So, how come Mom didn't tell me you'd be in town?"

"She doesn't know I'm here."

There's a pause at that.

"I definitely intended to look you up," Jack says directly to Emily. "Actually, I'd like to have a talk with you."

"Well," she says brightly, "bring the family and come on over after this and we'll all have some coffee and cake."

"By all means," adds Alan, taking out his card. "I'll write down the address. We're close by."

Jack lowers his voice. "Let's plan to do that very soon, but first, I'd like a private talk at Emily's convenience."

Emily pales. "Is something wrong?" Expecting the worst. "With my mother?"

Alan protectively puts his arm around his wife.

"I'm sorry," Jack says. "I'm handling this clumsily. I didn't mean to alarm you. Gladdy is fine. Busy with a new case."

Emily smiles, relieved. "That sounds like my mom."

"I need to talk to you about the past. When your father died. If you'd be willing to do that."

Her face shows her puzzlement. She hesitates, then says, "Of course. When would you like to meet?"

"Tonight, if that's all right with you."

Alan and Emily exchange startled looks. "Tonight?"

"I can take the kids home," Alan volunteers.

She nods. "Jack, there's a deli right on Amsterdam, stays open pretty late."

"Too bad Zabar's isn't open."

Everybody's favorite deli. They all smile, the tension broken.

"Twenty minutes?" Emily asks. "After I pay my respects to the devoted teacher who's stuck with all these rambunctious kids."

"I'll be there. Thank you." As he starts to walk away he turns and sees Emily and Alan look at one another. He hears Alan say, "You'll be all right?"

Emily nods. "I'm nervous. But I'm curious, too."

12

JACK AND EMILY

The deli is open, but getting ready to close. The two rather hefty brothers who own the shop—and obviously indulge greatly in their own products—are busily putting perishables away, chatting as they do. This deli features black-and-white photos on the walls, mostly daytime soap stars and the like. The tables have red-and-white checkered tablecloths and there is a jukebox playing the oldies-but-goodies of the sixties. Frank Sinatra is singing "My Way."

Emily and Jack sit in an old-fashioned wooden booth made of very dark oak that's been stained over and over again to maintain the gloss. They have coffee and pie in front of them. They barely touch their food. The greenish aura of the fluorescent lights make the room seem bleak. They are the only customers.

"Don't rush," one of the brothers assures them. "We got plenty left to do." With that he heads back to the storeroom, carrying a tray loaded with pastries.

"I apologize again for having scared you," Jack says. "I just didn't know how to go about this. I wasn't sure whether a phone call out of the blue would have been better or worse."

Emily looks skittish. And rightly so. Go slow, he tells himself. He's a stranger to her, after all.

"So you tracked me down at the school. Mom did tell me that you'd been a policeman in New York. Old techniques for catching people off their guard?"

She's smart, he thinks, just like her mother. "That's it. Not very nice of me. Would you believe me if I admitted feeling nervous about meeting you?"

"But this is very important to you or you wouldn't have done it. May I ask the obvious question?"

"You mean why didn't I tell Gladdy that I intended to see you?" He pauses. "She doesn't even know I'm in New York."

He can sense she's struggling to understand what that actually means.

She keeps it light. "Cloak-and-dagger stuff?"

"Something like that. You know I care very much for your mother."

"She hinted at such." Emily smiles.

He smiles, too. She's looking him up and down, assessing what her mother sees in him. "But I can't get her to commit to a relationship with me." He grins. "I hate that word."

Emily plays with her teaspoon, stirring the coffee that she isn't drinking. "Over the years Mom met some nice men, but she refused to even consider the idea of replacing my dad. Psychology one-oh-one. A matter of misplaced loyalty."

"Or fear of getting left again."

"But you're different. I can tell from her phone calls. She really feels the same about you. Maybe the problem is her life is too comfortable and change is hard."

"That, too."

"Something else?"

"More Psychology one-oh-one. I think your mother never had closure after your father died. Another word I hate. It keeps her from moving forward."

Emily tenses. "And that's why you wanted me to talk about my father?"

Easy, go easy. He doesn't want to scare her into silence. Jack takes a moment to sip the now cold coffee, then pushes it away. "Yes," he says carefully.

"You mean what he was like? What kind of man he was? Surely Mom told you about him."

"That's not what I had in mind. I want to

question you about the terrible night your father died."

Abruptly, she sits up straighter in her chair. Her face tightens. For a moment she doesn't speak. "I didn't expect that. I mean, I was only eleven. What could I possibly know? What do you need to know for? It was a long time ago and what's the point?" She stops, seemingly surprised at her passionate outbreak.

"I'm sorry. I'm upsetting you. You don't have to do this."

She gropes in her purse for a tissue. "Funny, I haven't let myself think about it in years. I thought I buried the memories with him. I mean, when I first met Alan I told him everything and cried a lot, but dear God, life goes on. There are so many times that I think, in a Kodak kind of family moment, why isn't he here to see his wonderful grandchildren? He never saw me grow up. Or saw me married. Or saw that I had a career he'd be so proud of." Emily buries her face in the tissue and cries. Jack reaches over and gently touches her shoulder.

Finally she blows her nose and looks back at him. "Wow! Where did that come from?"

"Not all buried after all," he says tenderly.

"I guess not."

Emily takes a deep breath. "I'm all right now. Ask me what you want to know."

"Just talk. About that night."

She shivers, but after a few moments, she begins. "It was New Year's Eve. My birthday. Even so, Dad was late getting home from the university. Mom and I had been baking my cake. She told me Dad would be home any minute, knowing how eagerly I was waiting for my presents.

"From our window we could see him heading down the street toward our apartment house. He saw us and was about to wave."

Emily twirls a length of her hair nervously. She takes a deep breath. "He never did wave. Suddenly, there was a woman's scream. Dad stopped and looked toward the corner. He dropped his briefcase and ran around that corner down the alley. We heard my father's voice yell, 'Run, Patty.' Then we heard it. It was a gunshot. My mother ran out of our apartment."

She watched her mother from the window, running into the alley. There was a dreadful silence. She couldn't stand it anymore. She had to go downstairs and find out what happened. She was terrified. Why didn't her mother come out again and call out to her? "Nothing to worry about. False alarm."

"My mother disappeared around the corner and that's when I grabbed my coat and ran downstairs, too."

Emily stops to sip at her water. Her hands are shaking. The brothers are looking at them, as if trying to decide whether to interrupt and tell them it's closing time. They approach, pause, and then walk away, shrugging, leaving them alone again.

"You actually saw your father lying on the ground?"

"Yes."

"Mommy, what happened. Mommy?" A girl ran past her. She looked about seventeen. She was tall and very skinny. She looked panic-stricken, as if she didn't know where to run.

"Get back, Emmy, don't come in here," Gladdy shouted.

"I only saw his legs. His motionless legs on the ground. I moved a little closer and saw my mother down on her knees, covering him with her body."

For a moment she thought her daddy was still alive; his body was shaking. But, no, it was her mother's body, racked with tears. Moaning hopelessly.

The girl who must have been Patty ran out of the alley toward some bushes near a wall and threw up. She pounded her fists against the brick, as if trying to hurt herself.

Emily's voice lowers as if it takes too much energy to speak. "I saw the girl, Patty, leaning against the brick wall, shrieking. Then I saw my father's briefcase where he'd dropped it."

She found herself walking over to it. She sat down on the cement and clutched it in her arms, rocking. Then she realized its contents had fallen out. She saw her father's notepapers. And her birthday present. He hadn't had a chance to wrap it yet. Of course it was a book. She always got books on her birthday. It was always a book her parents loved when they were growing up. This year it was Captain Horatio Hornblower. *The story of a very brave man.*

Emily pauses. She's choked up and having trouble speaking. "That was it. The end of my childhood, the end of ever enjoying a birthday again, and the end of my mother's life as she had known it."

Jack feels awful, but he has to make her go on. He's already learned something new—that she was a witness to much of this. His instincts are telling him she knows something more. Something she has never told before. His voice is quiet. "Emily, what happened next?"

"People heard the commotion. A crowd gathered, staring at the tragedy before them. By then my mother was screaming for a doctor. The police came."

"You never saw the killer? Nor did your mom?"

"No, the killer must have run down the other end of the alley. Later I was told that poor girl went crazy right after it happened."

"So the records say. She couldn't remember any of it. Her mind had blocked it out."

"And that was that. The police never caught whoever murdered my father."

The brothers are making it obvious that they are ready to close for the night. They start turning off lights and looking at their customers, shrugging.

Jack tosses some money on the table and leads Emily out the door.

It's still sticky and humid. By now the streets are dark and empty. Most lights are off in the apartment buildings. There's an occasional shout from some older kids prowling the neighborhood. A cat meows loudly at some nocturnal happening.

Jack walks Emily home. "Thank you for putting yourself through it again. I know how difficult it has to be for you."

She nods, still caught up in the emotion. Jack takes her arm and stops her. "You know, there's nothing in the files about you having been on the scene. Did the police ever question you?"

That catches her by surprise. "No, they never did. I guess because I was only a kid, and what could I possibly contribute?"

They stand in front of a darkened doorway. "Then I have a question for you. You said Patty ran past you. Did she say anything?"

"No, she was only crying. . . ."

Patty leaned against the building as if she needed it to hold her up. Emily thought the girl was going to faint. Patty seemed to become aware of someone watching her. She gasped, as if guessing who Emily was. Patty stared at her, then looked away, looking stricken. Moments later she turned back again. Her mouth opened to speak.

She reached out to Emily for a moment, and then dropped her arms.

Emily's eyes widen. "Wait a minute, she did say something. But I could hardly hear her, her voice was so low."

Jack is drawn in, intrigued. "What did she say?"

Emily shakes her head, agitated. "I don't remember. Please, how can I?"

"Try. You've been so helpful already, making me see the scene clearly through your eyes. But Emily, I think when something so traumatic happens to a person, all the senses are sharpened at those moments. Stop a moment and put yourself back in that time when she ran past you. Concentrate. Think of what you were feeling. What was going on around you? Try to remember anything."

She closes her eyes, unaware of a couple walking by. Jack holds his breath.

"My mother was shouting for a doctor. Patty was crying. I could feel my own tears and my nose dripping as I sobbed, too. I was aware of windows opening and lights going on. . . . Somebody's dog started barking. Wait."

With her eyes shut, Emily concentrates hard.

Patty was speaking to her, but she couldn't hear her for the blood rushing to her head. Emily said to her, "My father is dead . . . leave me alone. . . ." Patty's lips moved. Emily tried to listen. What was she saying? What? "My fault."

Emily's eyes spring open. " 'My fault.' That's what she said to me. 'My fault.' "

"Yes," Jack says triumphantly.

"Why?" Emily asks in anguish. "Why did you make me go through this again?"

Jack holds her hands in his. "Emily, I want to tell you something. The reason I've come up here is to find your father's killer."

It takes a moment for what he is saying to register. "But . . . but that's impossible. It's so long ago. . . ."

"I feel I have to try. For your mother's sake. Maybe for yours."

Gladdy's daughter throws herself into Jack's arms, her body shaking with sobs, and he holds her close.

13

JACK REPORTS
TO MORRIE

My fault?' That's all Patty Dennison said?" Morrie repeats what his father has just told him. "Funny how none of the police picked up on the fact she'd run downstairs after her mother and was actually at the crime scene."

"I wouldn't be surprised if Gladdy kept that information from them in order to protect her from being badgered. Or in the depth of their grief, she actually didn't think about it. And nobody asked."

Once again, Jack is in his hotel room, sitting on the one bilious green uncomfortable chair. He can picture Morrie cooking himself some dinner and listening with the phone tucked between his ear and shoulder as he moves about his kitchen.

"So, Wolfgang Puck, what am I missing tonight?" Jack asks.

"Nothing too fancy. Just some brook trout in lemon and clarified butter. With a soupçon of parsley and dill. Asparagus spears au gratin along with it."

Jack moans. "Don't rub it in. I ate a horrible hamburger in this dump's so-called coffee shop. I'm having Tums for dessert."

"Too lazy to find a healthier place? Dad, just because you live alone, you don't have to eat poorly."

Jack laughs. "Again with the lecture? I'm miles away from you and still you nag. Besides, I can't eat at Lisa's every night."

"I'm putting my brook trout in the oven. Eat your heart out. So how are you interpreting what Patty Dennison said?"

"First the obvious." Jack pulls his socks off and wiggles his toes. "She felt it was her fault Jack Gold was dead. He heard her cry out and ran to help her. If she hadn't done that, he'd still be alive."

"Or not. And if he hadn't, she might be dead."

"Perhaps it was a robbery—if she'd given the perp her purse, he would have run off."

"Or it might have been worse. It might have been an attempted rape. Or some psychopath. And he did have the gun. Maybe he intended to kill her. Too bad she wasn't able to talk about it afterward."

The room is stifling. Jack walks over to the air-conditioning unit and presses the start button. He waits. Nothing happens. Why isn't he surprised? "What keeps going through my mind is the shooting itself. Did he kill Gold because he was startled when Gold ran into the alley and he just reacted by pulling the trigger? Why not just run away? Why didn't he shoot Patty, too? He had to assume she might be able to recognize him in a lineup."

"Panic? Because Jack showed up? No time?"

"Could be. But a different idea runs around in my head. What if 'my fault' meant something entirely different? Her never being able to make a statement was a little too pat. What if she knew the guy?"

"There's a thought. Odd. The file doesn't mention any follow-ups on her later. Too many cases, too little time?"

"Well, this retired cop has plenty of time, and I think I'd like to interview Patty Dennison, wherever she is now." Jack heard a *ping*. "What's that?"

"My asparagus is ready for its au gratin sauce. Enjoy your Tums, Dad."

"You owe me the identical dinner when I get home just because you took such pleasure in tormenting me."

"Maybe I will and maybe I won't." He laughs. "I wonder if after all these years Patty's memory has returned. Assuming she's still alive somewhere."

"Then why didn't she come forward?"

"That is the question, isn't it?"

After a few more trivialities, they hang up. Jack pauses, still holding his cell phone, debating whether to call Gladdy.

14

THE LIBRARY

Ida is with me at the library, which is unusual. None of the girls ever want to go. They always leave it up to me to return their finished books and pick up new ones. I think Ida feels sorry for me; what with Evvie not wanting to do much of anything these days, Ida's trying to keep me company. This morning one of the neighbors asked Evvie when they'd see her next movie review. For that matter, our weekly newsletter, which Evvie puts out for all to read, has also stopped. She shrugged and said she was busy right now. What am I going to do with her?

We divide the book-picking job. With five lists in hand, one for each of us, naming all the books we've already read over the years—a huge list it is—we travel down the aisles. Before we started these lists, we ended up taking out the same books over and over, thanks to our failing senior memories. But we do read a lot and it is impossible to remember all the titles. Or authors. Sophie's comment is apt when she says that our memories are so bad, we don't remember a word about the books we've read. We might as well read the same books and enjoy them all over again.

Ida is tackling best-sellers for herself, and for Bella, romance novels in large print. I'm checking family-type sagas for Sophie and mysteries for me. Evvie, still in her funk, didn't want any new books, but I'm going to pick out a good one for her anyway. Something's got to bring her back to normal one of these days.

Ida and I pass one another. Her book bag is already full. "Goody, goody," she says, "I've got the latest Jodi Picoult. I've read them all; I love her stuff."

I smile. I'm pretty happy, too. "I've just grabbed the newest Charles Todd." His mystery series about England during the First World War makes for great reading.

My librarian friend, Conchetta, greets us when she gets a break. I always love the way she dresses. She wears wonderful Cuban fabrics and styles. Even though she's thirty-eight and chubby, her outfits make her look happy and friendly. Which she is. "Hello, happy campers. Good to see you again. Recovered from the wealthy life?"

Ida sniffs. "Too rich for my blood."

"Quite a big deal. It made all the papers."

"I'm just glad the police kept our names out of it. It's bad enough everybody at our condo knows we were involved. They're driving us crazy."

Conchetta wants to know, "Is Evvie okay?"

"Not yet," I inform her.

Ida says, "I'm glad our new case is a small one and won't involve murder."

I agree. "Come to think of it, 'Chetta, maybe you can help. We need to look someone up on the computer, if they're even on it."

Conchetta pretends to be miffed. "Why don't you go back to those Gossip girls? They have all the sleek, lightweight, up-to-date equipment." Naturally I have told Conchetta about the minimalist all-white office in the middle of a strip mall and the unusual cousins, Barbi and Casey, who run it.

"Nah, we're talking small potatoes. I wouldn't bother them for this."

"Well," she says, "at least I'm good for something, even if it's low tech."

We smile at one another. She's such a good friend.

As she sits at the console, running the name of Linda Silverstone, she says, "When are you going to get your own computer? You can do all your own Internet searches at home."

"No, thanks."

Ida adds, "Besides, our apartments are so small, we have no room."

"And further besides," I add, "I'm too old to learn new tricks."

"Nonsense," says Conchetta. "Get a laptop; they don't take up any room. And you're not too old. You'll have fun with it. You can even do your beloved crossword puzzles on it. Hey, you can even read up on people you know, even about yourselves."

"You're kidding," I say.

Conchetta grins and types Gladys Gold into the Google box. Ida and I look over her shoulder as she scrolls down name after name. I'm amused. There are so many people with my same name. Suddenly I stare in shock. There's *my* name. And facts about me. The award I won for New York Librarian of the Month way back in 1972. A conference I chaired at a librarian convention in '78. And more.

As she continues down the screen, I gasp. There are actually newspaper articles about my husband Jack's murder. I feel my cheeks redden, and my head immediately starts to ache. My heart pounds so loud in my chest I would swear Conchetta and Ida can hear it. Images rush through my brain, images I've purposely repressed all these years.

"How dare they? Who gives them permission to write about me?" I am enraged.

Conchetta looks at me with concern. "Welcome to the global network. And to the end of privacy as we know it. I'm sorry, Glad. I was being glib. I thought you knew about this."

Ida gets defensive. "Well, don't look me up. I don't want to know what's there. If anything." She actually looks panic-stricken.

I try to pull myself back together. "I thought only celebrities and people of importance or wealth would be written up. I would never have guessed that anyone in the world could be listed. And that anyone in the world could read about me if they wanted. I actually thought Linda Silverstone would be listed only if she was well known."

"You look pale. Do you want me to get you some water?" Conchetta asks.

"No. I'm all right." I manage a weak smile. "Now I know I've lived too long."

Ida gently swats me on the shoulder. "Pooh, pooh," she says, waving her hands as if to ward off evil spirits. "You should never say things like that."

That makes me smile. "I was kidding. I didn't know you were superstitious."

Ida huffs. "Well, now you know, so don't tempt the devil."

Conchetta is abashed. "Do you still want me to Google Linda Silverstone?"

I shrug, trying to play down how upset I really am. "Even though I've sprung three new gray hairs in the last five minutes, carry on. I do want to know about Linda."

"She's there. And it lists her website. I'll take us to that." Conchetta does something magical and we are looking at a page with Linda's name on the top.

"I can't believe it," Ida says. "Not only is she on a list, she also has her own pages to talk about herself? On purpose?" She shakes her head in disbelief.

"Never mind," I say, "let's see what she says about herself. Her age is sixty. Is nothing sacred? Single. She's a well-known author. Writes nonfiction. Her books are listed. So is her education. Linda has a Ph.D. from Stanford. Her field is Public Health. She's a known dietitian. She has an office in Miami, The Health Wellness Mystical Connection. She is the daughter of Dr. Harvard Elmore Silverstone."

Conchetta looks up. "I've heard of her father." She scrolls down. "Yes, here it is, he became something of a health guru in the seventies. His book, *The Joke's on Death*, was a runaway bestseller."

I nod. The librarian in me remembers it. "Wasn't his thesis that by positive thinking you can prevent and/or cure physical illness?"

"And his daughter Linda followed in his footsteps," Conchetta added.

Ida says, "Wait a minute, wasn't he considered some kind of crank?"

Conchetta nods. "Yes, there was a lot of controversy about his theories. I'll bet we have both their books here."

So when I leave, my book bag is even fuller.

I now have a collection of the works of Drs. Harvard and Linda Silverstone to research.

But seeing my own name in the computer has upset me dreadfully. Once again my mind has been forced to think about the sadness in my past. And I hate it. When will I ever be free?

15

NEW YEAR'S EVE 1961

SISTERS

For a moment Emily thought she was crying snow. The tiny snowflakes touched her face and they mingled with her tears. She no longer felt the cold of the cement beneath her. She no longer felt anything. But she was aware of everything. As if she were sitting on a stage and a play was unfolding. It must have been—it couldn't be happening in her real life.

People exited and entered the stage. First were the neighbors, hurrying toward the alley. Peering in fearfully, then withdrawing, shocked and reaching for others for comfort. As if they were glad it wasn't them?

Emily felt something tickling her bare leg. She glanced down and saw her father's papers raised by the wind, drifting away. She shut the briefcase, *thinking he'd be upset with her when he found out his notes were lost. From her vantage point she stared again at his feet pointed downward.* Why doesn't he get up?

One of their neighbors, Mrs. Brownstein from the ninth floor, was coming toward her. Emily shook her head frantically, her hands pushed out, demanding she keep away. The woman paused, then, teary-eyed, retreated.

The ambulance arrived, its red lights zigzagging across the near-darkened buildings. Grabbing their medical gear, the rescuers jumped out and ran into the alley. From out of nowhere a newspaper reporter appeared, carrying a huge Speed Graphic, snapping photos. The whites of the flash mingled with the reds of the ambulance.

Why doesn't my mother get up? *Emily asked herself, as she saw the men trying to lift her mother off her father's body. She became aware that her mother wore only a sweater.* She must be so cold. Like Daddy, so cold.

Her mother fought them, trying to shove the three young men away with what little strength she had. But they pulled her up easily and she lost her grip on Jack's coat.

The reporter moved close to her side and spoke softly, but her mother covered her ears in order not to hear his words.

The medical team was trying to determine if her father was still alive. Her mother could tell them that, Emily thought. Her mother knew everything about him, even to the way his breath sounded. But Emily could see his breath was gone. Her father was gone.

Why didn't her mother scream?

The reporter supported her mother and helped her out of the alley. It was then she saw Emily. She pulled away and ran to her daughter. Emily dragged herself up off the ground and fell into her arms. Both of them were shivering.

"He's dead. Daddy's dead." Her mother repeated the words over and over again.

Emily kept crying "No," as if trying to change what she knew she couldn't.

"What is it?" They heard a woman shriek. "What happened?"

Then the three of them, Evvie, Joe, and their daughter, Martha, huddled in their winter coats, were at their side, trying to take in what was going on. Seeing it all at once. Paramedics working over Jack. Gladdy and Emily clutching one another. Onlookers encircling them, but not too closely, as if death were something catching.

Joe looked down the alley, and then at Gladdy. "Oh, no, not Jack," he said. In the distance the police sirens were heard.

The sisters stared into one another's eyes.

It can't be, Evvie's eyes said.

It is, Gladdy said without a sound.

They never needed words with one another.

What was there to say? Gladdy's life, as she had known it, had just ended.

Cousin Martha, twelve years old and the image of her redheaded mother, stared at Emily, hardly understanding. Emily ran to her and hugged her. It was hard to do; Martha's arms were full of gaily wrapped birthday presents.

"Someone shot my father," she told her. Martha dropped the birthday presents and started to bawl.

Gladdy turned to the girls. "Emmy, please take your cousin upstairs."

Neither one could move.

Uncle Joe, a shock of thick black hair falling over his forehead, bent down. He was nose to nose with them, his voice gruff. "Did you hear your mother? Both of you—get out of here!"

They ran.

16

A MOTHER CALLS

A lovely time is being had by all. The Gold/
Levinson family and the Langford/Berman
clan are just finishing dinner in the tasteful
Amish-style dining room. Jack sits back, absorbing everything. They are in Emily and Alan's
apartment, only five blocks from where his own
daughter Lisa's family lives, on the west side of
the city. The apartment is charming and cozy,
filled with gentle clutter and comfortable, relax-
ing furnishings. He is not surprised. Emily has
Gladdy's warmth and liveliness about her. The
family interests abound. They like art and the
walls are filled with original works of New York
artists they favor. The den contains the family
archives. Photos of Emily and Alan Levinson
and their three daughters and one son skiing and

snorkeling and hiking. Lots of travel snapshots. And family occasions like birthday parties. And Grandma Gladdy grins down at her children and grandchildren in many of them.

These are two fine families. *Hopefully,* Jack thinks, *someday soon both will be related by the marriage of us two oldsters.* And what a plus: They already like one another. All the kids seem to hit it off. Eleven-year-old Jeremy, especially, is in heaven, being at eleven-year-old Lindsay's house. Lindsay, with her curly reddish brown hair and face full of freckles, looking sweet in pink, has obviously dressed up for him.

Earlier, fifteen-year-old Patrick showed thirteen-year-old Jeffrey the cartoons he'd drawn. He hopes to make it big in that field. Jeffrey is impressed with this boy, two years older than he is, who already has career plans. The missing Levinson children are Elizabeth and Erin, twenty-one and nineteen, respectively, both away at college. Jack already knows about them—Gladdy boasted like a good grandma should—but he listens again patiently as the proud parents report that Elizabeth is majoring in dance, with a focus on ballet, while Erin is studying to be a vet.

The husbands immediately find they have much in common: Alan, a doctor; Dan, a lawyer. At one point they get into a spirited conversation about medical liability laws. The women have their careers to discuss, as well. Emily is a school counselor; Lisa is a clinical psychologist. They, too, have a lot to share with one another. There is much exchanging of war stories. Lots of good wine flowing. Laughter. A perfect evening.

Only one thing is missing: Gladdy. Her name comes up over and over with "I wish Mom were here," from Emily, and "I wish she were, too," from everyone else. And on all the adults' minds is the reason Jack is in New York.

Jack knows he will get hell from Gladdy when she finds out. How could he have done this without her? He feels plenty guilty about it. Not only has he arranged this behind her back, he hasn't even called to let her know. Even worse, he's already asked her family to keep his presence here a secret, making them all feel uncomfortable. It's left unsaid this evening, but all of them know how much is at stake.

The lemon chicken with wild rice is a big success, but Emily's homemade blueberry cheesecake is the topper. By the time they are having coffee, the kids are already immersed in the TV. Baby Molly sleeps sweetly in her carrier.

The phone rings. Emily, still laughing, goes into the kitchen to answer. From the dining room, they hear her say, suddenly loudly, "Mom. What a pleasant surprise."

All talking stops. They can all see her from

where they are sitting. "How are you?" Emily asks.

"Just fine, that's good." Emily can tell she's lying. "I'm so glad you called, Mom. I was thinking of you tonight." Jack looks at her. Emily shrugs as if to say, well, aren't we, as a matter of fact.

"The kids? The kids are good." Emily blanches. She closes her eyes and says carefully, "I know they'd love to talk to you, but they have play dates over. Should I disturb them?"

Emily feels miserable. She knows the kids wouldn't be able to keep their secret. She gives Jack a woeful look. Jack bows his head. He's causing her family to lie for a man they hardly know.

"No, I'm not busy," Emily continues. "Just finishing dinner. I made my favorite one of your recipes, the lemon chicken.... Yes, lots of onions.... I'm glad you called, Mom.... I'll talk to you again in a few days."

Emily hangs up.

There's a chilly silence. Jack stands when she returns to the dining room. "I'm so sorry." Their discomfort is clear. "I think I'd better leave now."

Lisa and Dan get up, too.

Jack tries to stop them. "Please, no, stay. I don't want to spoil the party. Please."

Lisa insists, "Your grandchildren need their sleep."

A chorus of "No, not yet" comes from the happy, wide-awake kids in the living room.

There's an exchange of good nights.

Emily walks Jack to the door. She kisses him on the cheek. "My father was a hero. I think you're one, too."

Jack manages a weak smile and leaves.

17

FINALLY A LEAD

Jack waits in the back of the Carnegie Deli on Seventh Avenue. It has always been a favorite of his even though the seats are cramped together and diners are forced to sit, practically touching shoulders, with total strangers. The aisles behind the seats are so narrow the waiters have to hang over the customers to serve them their meals. Sometimes a hot plate of food comes dangerously close to causing a calamity, but even though they are always moving fast, those waiters never miss. At least as far as he knows, they haven't.

In the old days it was a big hangout for the famous stars of the New York theaters. Their black-and-white photos still crowd every inch of every wall. Many look old and faded. Now the restaurant exists mostly for tourists. And the prices reflect it. To give them a reason for the astronom-ical prices, the size of a typical sandwich could feed a family of seven. A human mouth couldn't open wide enough to get a full bite. But it's a trip down memory lane for Jack, so it's worth it.

Jack orders a diet tuna salad plate. In the old days that order would have prompted derision from one of the big burly waiters. "What are you—a wuss?" Now, no one cares. Everything changes, Jack thinks with a sigh.

It's ten-thirty A.M. Just after the breakfast crowd and slightly before lunch. Sitting in the very last row of adjoining tables, he figures he has a little time before it gets crowded. He takes out his file again with his notes on Patty Dennison. Hoping if he rereads, maybe he'll find something he missed.

There's a contact number for Patty's family, so old it still has two letters in front of the numbers. MU. He remembers; that was a Murray Hill ex-change, but the letters are long gone.

Detective Tim Reilly arrives. "Glad you could make it," Jack says.

"Yeah, but why here? I can't afford this place."

"For old time's sake. Eat light."

"Shucks, and I thought you were treating me." They both laugh. "Anything useful in the files?"

"Nothing much."

"That's a really cold trail, buddy."

"I know. But I have to try."

"You might be in luck. I got a lead for you.

There was a newspaper guy worked for the *Daily News* back then—Milt Paxton? Do you recall?"

"Rings a bell. Wasn't he a reporter who used to drive everybody crazy? Is he still around?"

"Sort of."

Jack feels this could be something. But he doesn't want to get his hopes up.

The waiter comes over, pad in hand. Tim orders a pastrami, bacon, and turkey sandwich on rye with Thousand Island dressing, with fries and onion rings.

"That's your idea of light?"

"*You* said light. I didn't say I agreed. Besides, I get to eat the leftovers for three days."

"What about Paxton?"

"I remembered he was hot on your lady friend's case. The word was he kept trying to follow the Dennison girl around to get her story. In fact he was such a pest, her family got a restraining order. He might have a notion where she went." With that Tim takes out a scrap of paper with a phone number. "He's living with a niece on Long Island. Hopefully he still has all his marbles."

"Behind," warns a hoarse Brooklyn accent, and both men know this is the magic word telling them to duck. Waiter behind them, with hands and arms full of plates.

Tim's order has arrived, and he and Jack watch how expertly the waiter extricates his food from the five other orders adorning his arms.

Jack shakes his head at the enormity of Tim's portion, then goes back to eating his salad. "You'll be sorry later."

"I know. I'm already sorry." Tim chomps hard on the sandwich, the dressing spilling sloppily over the sides. He leans over fast so he won't ruin his suit. Jack laughs again.

Suddenly there's a rush of people hurrying in, grabbing for seats. Through the window Jack can see that they're exiting a huge tour bus.

Tim starts wrapping his sandwich, at the same time signaling the waiter for the check. "There goes the neighborhood. Let's blow this joint and eat in the park."

So much for memory lane.

18

A MAN LOST FOREVER

Jack hops off the Long Island Railroad line and follows the directions Milt Paxton gave him over the phone. The station is within walking distance of an older neighborhood in Syosset, tree-lined, probably once a nice middle-class neighborhood, now gone downhill. The houses look old and neglected.

It was evident that Paxton wanted company. He refused to talk on the phone. So here Jack is, heading for a guy who might know something. Probably a wild-goose chase. But once again, he's going on instinct. For years, this reporter hadn't given up trying to reach Patty for a story. Even though she was incapable of speech? Jack wants to know why he persisted for so many years.

When he reaches the address, he sees a man

104 • Rita Lakin

sitting in a wheelchair on the porch—Milt, eagerly waiting for him. On a bench next to him are opened scrapbooks. Jack bets that Milt spent the time until the train came in gathering his old articles on the case.

Milt Paxton is in his eighties. His thin, small body doesn't seem to move much, but his gaunt face lights up when Jack climbs the rickety steps.

"Guess how many years it's been since somebody came to see me? Guess. Never, that's the answer." That's Paxton's greeting to him. Before Jack can speak, Paxton yells, "Maria!"

A harried, stringy-haired, scrawny woman about twenty years younger than Paxton hurries out with a tray holding lemonade and cookies. "I was coming out. Hold your horses, you mean old man."

She introduces herself as Milt's niece. "Thanks to this old codger, I have no life. Stay a long time and give me some peace!" With that she flounces back into the house, slamming the screen door after her.

Milt Paxton chuckles. "Don't mind her. She loves waiting on me hand and foot."

"I can see that," Jack says wryly, sitting down on the rocker next to him.

Paxton points to his scrapbooks. "It's all there, the Jack Gold killing. I was on it from the beginning." Jack glances at the articles. There are Milt's bylines, accompanied by photos taken on the scene. There's Gladdy, holding onto her husband, refusing to let go as the EMTs try to get her to stand up. It was one thing to read the files, another to see these vivid photos.

He can't take his eyes off the younger Gladdy, in her early thirties, on that dreadful day. For a moment, in his mind, he's there with her, feeling her pain. He pulls himself back to now. "I was told you kept trying to talk to Patty Dennison."

"Oh, yeah, I was on her like a tick on a dog. But once they whisked her away to the hospital, it got tougher. The cops weren't letting anybody near."

"The files say she went into shock, couldn't speak, and when she could, didn't remember anything."

"Yeah, sure. That was the story the family gave out. I thought different."

Jack sips at the lemonade and winces at how sour it is. "Why? What made you think that?"

"You know, those days we'd do anything for a hot story. You smelled a story, you went after it. These no-talents today wait 'til it's e-mailed to them." He spits, missing Jack's shoe by inches. "I snuck into the hospital after midnight, grabbed a janitor's coat and mop out of the storeroom, and made my way upstairs. There was a cop by the door of Dennison's room. I mopped in and out of all the rooms. Thank God none of the nurses came by. When I got to her door, the cop was snoozing. I mopped my way in. Patty's mother was sitting by her side. They were talking real quiet. Yeah, my hunch was right; the girl who couldn't talk was a liar. The mom said, 'We'll go up to Auntie Leona's house, 'til it all blows over.' Patty was crying. 'It won't be far enough,' the girl said.

"Then the mom noticed me. 'Get out!' she said. 'Now!' The cop ran in. I kept my head down low and backed out. That girl was as coherent as you or me."

Jack looks at him, excited. "Then what?"

"Then I did everything I could to get to her. Even followed her up to Fair Lawn in New Jersey, where she had family. That's when they threw the restraining order at me. I knew damn well she was hiding the truth. I even went after her family. I went to where they worked, where they shopped, but boy, their mouths were closed with glue."

"Did you ever get to talk to her?"

"No."

"Why not?" Jack asks, disappointed.

"I got hit by a truck."

Jack looks at Paxton as if he is pulling his leg.

"A truck carrying toilet paper. Hit right in the middle of Fair Lawn's main drag. A stupid accident because I wasn't looking where I was going. Ain't that a kick in the head? Paralyzed me; been in a chair since then. That was the end of my career. You think I'd ever forget Patty Dennison?"

Jack doesn't know what to say.

Maria comes back out, hearing his last words. She puts her arms tenderly around her uncle's shoulder, and he leans into her. She looks at Jack sadly. "That's enough to make a man mean, wouldn't ya say?"

"I'm sorry," Jack says to Paxton.

"Yeah, life's a bitch and then you die. Some famous depressed writer who lived with his mother wrote something like that. Just as bad as living with a miserable, ungrateful niece."

Maria leans over his shoulder and gives him a kiss.

He smiles sheepishly at Jack. "Kinfolks. But I kept track of Miss Patty. I knew where she was— until suddenly I didn't. She disappeared. By then I was so deep in a world of pain, I didn't give a rat's ass about her anymore." Thirsty now, he sucks at the straw in his glass of lemonade on the table. His niece reaches over and holds the glass steady for him. When he finishes, she wipes his chin, smiles, and goes back inside.

"Your turn, Langford. Why are you here?" Now appears the sharp-eyed glance of the reporter he once was. "Why so suddenly interested in a very cold case?"

"I hope to solve it. I want to marry Jack Gold's widow, and my wedding present to her will be the solution of this crime."

For a moment Milt looks at him, and then starts laughing so hard, he begins to cough. "Hot damn!" he says. "You're nuttier than I am."

Jack is not amused.

"You really mean it? You didn't come out here

'cause some old buddy of mine sent you to pull my chain?"

"Tell me everything you know. Who was Patty's family in New Jersey? Who was hiding her? Who knew what she knew and wasn't telling? I want to pick your brains until they're dry."

For a moment, Milt says nothing, then he begins to cackle. "You really mean it, you dumb son of a bitch. Okay, I'll give you everything I got. But you gotta promise me something."

"Name it."

"Whatever you find, you share with me."

"Done."

"Who knows, I might win that Pulitzer after all." He manages to wheel his chair a little closer to the front door. He yells again through the screen. "Maria, put another plate on the table, we got company for dinner! And try for once to cook something better than pig slop!"

Jack leans back in his rocker and waits to hear what Paxton has to offer.

19

STAKEOUT

I can't believe I stayed up half the night reading the Silverstone books in bed. Or rather skimming. There were a lot of charts and graphs and testimonials, typical for that genre of book, but the gist of it was that Linda's daddy, Harvard, originally from England, belonged to the stiff-upper-lip school of dealing with illness. Kind of like you're ill only if you think you're ill. He was into the power of suggestion and laughter as a cure-all, but mostly, it felt to me, it was denial. Refuse to accept your illness and make it go away. Something like that.

I get up to my usual routine. Put the coffeepot on, get one slice of rye bread and toast it. Then lightly butter. I glance as always at my crossword puzzle, halfway done by now, but my mind isn't into games. I'm into real puzzles. Like what's up with Linda Silverstone and her folks.

Daughter Linda, I guess, followed in Daddy's footsteps. They've been in the same business for years. They collaborate on books. They each run health clinics in different cities. Seems like the family is close. So why won't their daughter attend their very important anniversary party? What's wrong with this picture?

I look up the address of her clinic and wait until ten A.M. to give them a call.

A male voice answers. I ask for Dr. Linda Silverstone.

"State your business." The male voice is decidedly cool.

This throws me. I am about to say it's personal. But I have a different idea. "I'd like to set up an appointment with her. At her earliest convenience."

There's a long pause. Then, "Dr. Silverstone no longer does consultations. Can I set you up with someone else in the office?"

That's a surprise. Another try. "Well, I did have my heart set on her. I read Dr. Silverstone's books...."

"I'm sure anyone else on our staff will do. We are all partners in the same medical care program."

I guess I'll have to try another approach. "I really need to see her. It's personal."

Now the silence is longer. This is getting weird.

The stuffy voice is back. "I'm sorry. Perhaps you would send her a letter stating your reason for your request. Do you have our address?"

This is getting me nowhere. I tell him I do and I hang up. Then I reason that maybe because of her books, she gets a lot of attention. She has someone screen her calls. I can understand that, but there's something in his tone that makes me suspicious. Something seems off.

First stop on our way to Linda's house is a large upscale mall not far from where we are going. Sophie and Bella can't wait to be dropped off. Since they did the original legwork, they feel they should be excused. They have visions of dress shops and delis dancing in their heads. They get out of the car, grab hands, and do a little jump up and down. Happily in their second childhood. I can't tell whether they're behaving like teenagers or two-year-olds.

"When should we pick you up, your royal highnesses?" Ida doesn't bother hiding her sarcasm, though it's lost on the two of them.

Bella is gleeful. "It sure beats that last stakeout we were on, at night on that awful street."

Sophie adds, "Yuk. Nothing to look at, nothing to buy."

"And no bathrooms anywhere." Bella shudders at the memory of the awful bar in Plantation, where we staked out a client's husband.

"Perhaps you might want to look into a hotel and stay overnight. And shop some more tomorrow as well." Icy-toned Ida still waits for a response.

"You're wasting your breath," I tell her. To the girls, I say, "Call us on the cell phone when you're ready to come back to work."

Bella feels a minuscule amount of guilt. "Do you want we should do takeout and get some sandwiches for you?"

Ida lets her off the hook. Sort of. "Don't bother, I love going hungry."

With that she and I drive away. "The little twits," Ida adds.

Ida is sitting next to me up front. Sister Evvie's place of honor. Need I say Evvie is not with us? Yet again another excuse to be left alone and wallow in self-pity.

The girls were right. Linda Silverstone's house is impressively large and elegant, in a mock-Tudor style. But clearly built with security in mind, set far back with a long driveway and fenced all around. There's an intercom at the entrance. We park across the street and settle in for a long wait.

I catch Ida up on my reading of last night. She pales at the mention of the library. I make an educated guess. "You were also weirded out about the Google search?"

"Yeah. I didn't like the idea of our lives being so easy to probe."

I know I shouldn't but I'm curious. "What did you think they'd say about you?"

Ida immediately stiffens. "Nothing," she says too quickly.

I'm sorry I asked. It's none of my business. If Ida wants to tell me something personal she'll get to it in her own time. "Sorry," I say.

My cell phone rings, startling Ida. "They can't have bought out the stores already."

"It might be Dr. Silverstone, the father. I put in a call this morning and left word for him to call me back." Sure enough it is. I introduce myself and Ida, who I tell him is standing by. I remind him they've already spoken. I turn up the sound and Ida leans over in order to listen in.

"What can I do to help you?" he asks. His voice is a rich baritone. I imagine him to be a good public speaker. From his book jackets I already know what he looks like: ramrod tall, lanky, thin. His wife, Elsbeth, as well. They look so much alike, they might have been brother and sister.

"Tell us your plans. We hope to talk to your daughter soon. It might help to know what she'll be missing."

"We have an elaborate shindig planned for the weekend. Guests will be flying in from all over the country. My university and business colleagues. And Linda's aunts and uncles as well. All of us will be staying at the Ritz-Carlton. There will be a cocktail party Friday night and golf Saturday morning. Saturday night, a banquet with fine dining and dancing, for Elsbeth's and my seventieth wedding anniversary. Sunday we're planning an all-day hike along the Everglades."

Ida and I look at one another, impressed. I ask, "Sounds quite vigorous. May I ask your ages?"

The doctor laughs. "I'm ninety-four and Elsbeth is a mere ninety-two. We practice what we preach in our books."

I think how upbeat and robust this man sounds.

Ida comments, "It certainly seems like it."

I ask, "Can you think of any possible reason your daughter doesn't want to join you on this important occasion?"

Elsbeth is now on the line. She sounds chirpy and optimistic as well. "Absolutely not. We're very close to our daughter and she always attends every family function. We do need your help to understand what is going on."

I ask, "Have you spoken to her lately?"

"No, she only e-mails. I mean that isn't unusual. We've been in the habit of doing that for years. But not to speak to us at all? What could she possibly be working on that she can't take off a weekend for us? We know she's writing a new book; she keeps us apprised, but still."

Harvard adds, "In fact she used to hop in her Mercedes and drive the hundred and fifty miles on a whim just to surprise us."

"We are greatly puzzled," Elsbeth says. Now

there is a quaver in her voice. "Did we do or say something that offended our daughter? We can't imagine what. I've always thought of us as a very close family."

Harvard continues. "Besides hurting our feelings, how can she insult all our guests, most of whom she's known all her life?" He pauses. "I won't beg."

Elsbeth says with passion, "I would. I need to have our daughter with us."

Ida nudges me. A car drives up to the gate.

I close the conversation. "We will do what we can and inform you as soon as we know something." The Silverstones thank us and we all hang up.

"I missed it," I say to Ida. "Did you see what was written on the side of the van?"

"I think it said something about gourmet foods."

The van is buzzed in. Ida grabs the binoculars and watches the front door. I squint to see as well. Sure enough it's a grocery delivery. A woman comes to the door, but it can't be Linda; this woman is much younger. She signs a receipt and the door closes. The van leaves.

"Well," says Ida, "that tells us she doesn't answer her own door or do her own shopping. She has an assistant or something, who doesn't do the shopping, either. Wonder if the woman lives in?"

"Linda and her parents sound like a loving family."

"Unless they're lying," says my cynical partner.

I muse. I wonder how Evvie would feel knowing that Ida has taken her place and is a pretty good assistant.

Nothing much happens in the hours we wait. Ida and I share our bag lunch. No one else arrives or leaves. I attempt to call Linda a few more times but still get the answering machine every time. We wait for her assistant to leave. She doesn't.

"Next time we come earlier and leave later," I inform Ida.

"Whatever."

Finally at seven o'clock I pick up my "helpers" at the mall. Their arms are filled with packages.

"Is it that late already?" Sophie comments. "My, how time flies when you're having fun."

Need I say a word?

20

FULL SPEED AHEAD

They sit in the lobby of Jack's seedy run-down hotel: Jack, his daughter, Lisa, and Gladdy's daughter, Emily. The lobby is a study in discolored browns and faded shades of beige. The lights are kept low, the better to hide what time has wrought on this sad place.

Despite what the place looks like, it is filled with tourists. Hotels are always at a premium in this city. The travelers look harried, mostly Europeans who trusted the descriptions of what they would find here from far away. The hotel staff, having seen it all, and been around too long, are bored and lethargic. Service is at a minimum.

Lisa is still needling Jack for not staying with her in their apartment on the West Side. "I guess my dad doesn't mind hot and cold running bugs."

She pretends to scratch her legs as if something is crawling. "This place gives new meaning to the word 'fleabag.' "

"Please," Jack retorts, "my abode is centrally located in the heart of Manhattan, where all the action is. Besides, I like beds that sag in the middle—keeps me from falling out."

Emily and Lisa laugh. "No accounting for some people's taste," Emily says.

Jack is practically *kvell*ing at the two women now becoming fast friends. After Back to School Night, they got together, he suspects, to gossip about their parents, probably speculating about their parents' love affair. He imagines them giggling behind his back.

Lisa has learned from Emily why her father has come back to New York, and now they're his cheering squad. Encouraging him on, breathlessly hoping he can do the impossible. Jack thinks he's crazy for undertaking such an unattainable goal, and even crazier for telling them about it.

Look at them, Lisa's blond head leaning into Emily's dark one, dressed like the sophisticated New Yorkers they are. Their eyes are bright with excitement—and worry, as well. Two beautiful, smart, caring women. Wait 'til Gladdy finds out. After she gets over wanting to kill Jack for doing this behind her back, she'll be as thrilled as he is.

For an hour they've been unaware of the people going back and forth with suitcases, the doors opening, the sound of the bellman's whistle summoning cabs; even the Musak piped in has no effect on them. So totally focused they are in listening as Jack gives them the details of how he intends to proceed with his impossible quest.

They are rat-a-tat questioning his every comment.

"How long will you be away?" Emily.

"I'm not sure yet."

"Is there someone there who can help you?" Lisa.

"Not really."

"Will you bring the police in on it?" Emily.

"Only when and if I have to."

"How do you expect to find her?" Lisa.

"What if Patty moved away?" Emily.

"What is she refuses to talk to you?" Lisa.

His hands fly up in mock reproach. "Whoa. Slow down. I promise to keep you up on what I find out. I have names of relatives, thanks to that oddball reporter, Milt Paxton. I have an old address. Believe me, if she's there, I'll track her down. And I will find a way to make her talk to me."

"When are you leaving?" Lisa asked.

"I'll pick up the car rental and head out as soon as we are done. It's not that far away. Maybe twenty minutes or so over the bridge. And I'll dig right in."

Almost in unison, the women lean back against the worn brown couch. He can almost feel their tension. "Try not to worry."

"Hahaha," says Lisa. "What, me worry?" mimicking Alfred E. Neuman, the *Mad* magazine character.

There is finally a lull in the conversation. It's as if they've run out of things to say. All that's left are the unmentionable fears and doubts.

Lisa stands up. "I've got to go and pick the baby up at the sitter." Emily stands, too. "I've got to stop at Gristedes for something for dinner."

The three of them head for the door. Outside, they respond momentarily to the heat and the crowds hurrying past them. The women take turns hugging Jack.

"Be careful," Lisa warns.

"Godspeed," Emily says.

Jack watches after them as they walk away from him.

He says a quiet prayer to himself: *Please don't let me fail.*

21

HEADING OUT

Jack is following his pal Tim Reilly's directions and warnings. Yes, the West Side Highway is full of potholes and, yes, there's plenty of traffic. He drives his rented Ford Escort onto the lower level of the George Washington Bridge. Tim advised him of the maze of confusing signs once he got off, but he finds the exit for Route 4 west easily enough. He passes Fort Lee and remembers taking his children to the Palisades Amusement Park, which no longer exists.

Such happy days. He and Faye would hold hands and watch as Morrie and Lisa went on those terrifying rides: The Tilt-A-Whirl, the Cyclone, the Wild Tiger—one more petrifying than the other. How they loved the excitement.

"Tell me when they're off," Faye would say, keeping her eyes closed until the kids were on the ground again. Those precious days when Jack took time off from work, hoping every moment that his beeper wouldn't ring and disrupt their day. Faye never stopped worrying. She dreaded the possibility that someday he would not come home at all. But God was good to them: Jack survived being a cop; Faye lived long enough to see their children grow up. He was a lucky man. Now he has a new chance at love. And this trip will bring his new love the best wedding present he can give her.

He passes Teaneck, then Hackensack. Finally he turns at his exit at Saddle River Road. It's only taken him half an hour to arrive at Fair Lawn, where he is determined to ferret out Patty Dennison. Or else. Or else what? he wonders. What if the trail ends here?

Jack watches the signs carefully. He's heard about Radburn, the unique model community built in the thirties, almost a town within a town. It has a park at its center, with the streets angling out at its hub, a contained unit.

But he senses that's not where he needs to go. He follows the road into Fair Lawn itself, past Carvel Ice Cream and Topps Cleaners and the Royal Bakery. As he starts leaving town, he sees a diner and a nearby motel. That should work. Register, and then hit the diner. He'll stir with a big spoon and let whatever relatives might still be around learn that a big gun is in town.

He has made the decision to stay here, at least overnight, to see what might happen. The motel is adequate, like so many chains across the country. He leaves his duffel bag there and walks across the way to the diner, his shirt clinging to him in the heat. His khakis are wrinkled from the drive. He enters the diner—it, too, is like thousands of others of its kind across the country.

It's lunchtime. Jack isn't hungry, having had a nosh with the girls. He orders coffee at the counter and looks around. It's what he would expect. A trucker type, probably from the rig parked right outside. A couple of moms with their small children. A few guys in suits, maybe from the real estate office he just passed. A man and woman casually dressed. A youngish redheaded male, alone, reading a newspaper. Good. Mostly locals. There's a low buzz of quiet conversation.

Jack takes out his map and pretends to study it: the ultimate tourist. The counter waitress, plain-looking and curious, wears a uniform with one of those old-fashioned napkins in her pocket with a name tag. Betty hands him a menu. "Looking for someplace?"

Jack smiles at her. "Actually looking for someone, Betty," he says, reading her tag. "She had family, used to live on Upton Street. Doubt they're there anymore."

"Maybe I could help you. Born and bred in Fair Lawn."

"Dennison. Patty Dennison?" he says, purposely raising his voice.

The chatter stops. The customers openly stare at him. Betty recoils. The owner, big and brawny, fiftyish, maybe once was a boxer, quickly steps forward from behind the counter, placing his bulk in front of the waitress, arms crossed. "Nobody in this town named Dennison."

"Her name's Patty? Maybe you knew her? Know where she moved to?"

"Never heard of her."

Jack turns to the other customers. "Anybody else know her? It's worth a few bucks." No one speaks. The customers pretend to concentrate on their meals. The redhead rattles his paper.

Jack purposely looks insincere, about to tell a lie that would easily not be believed. "She's got some money coming to her and I'm here to give it to her."

The owner looks at him in disgust. "Yeah, right." He returns to his griddle. The waitress moves away.

"What about anybody named Sutterfield? B. Sutterfield?" One of the family names from Paxton's list. Not a peep out of anyone. "I'm at the motel across the highway if anyone thinks of something. Jack Langford."

Jack downs the rest of his coffee, pays, and leaves the totally silent restaurant.

He walks around the corner and pretends to be looking at a newspaper rack. He doesn't have to wait long. It's the redheaded young man who was reading a newspaper.

"How much is this information worth?"

"Fifty bucks if it's true info."

The young man's hand snakes out. Jack holds the money away from him. "What do you know?"

"I know Barbara Sutterfield. We both work at the Nabisco factory."

"Why aren't you there now?"

"I get sick of eating in the cafeteria."

"Where's Patty? That's worth a hundred."

He hesitates, his eyes glued to Jack's open wallet. Jack notices his jeans are worn; his T-shirt advertises a local bowling alley. The young guy shakes his head as if to shake temptation away. "I only know about Barbara."

Jack pretends to get tough. "How do I know you're telling the truth?"

"My name's Dick Smiler." He indicates the coffee shop. "Everyone knows me."

"I'll find you if I have to."

Jack looks Smiler hard in the eyes for a few seconds, then hands him a crisp fifty. The young man starts moving away quickly. He turns. "You some reporter or something?"

Jack smiles. "Something."

The guy runs off to where his car is parked in

the back lot. Jack is pleased. *Go ahead, kid, tell the whole town.*

He buys the paper and crosses back to the motel, deciding on the way. He'll wait until tomorrow, let the word spread. Let the tension build. Maybe Paxton's information was still good and he caught a big break. Patty still has family here, and that's a very good omen.

22

GETTING TO LINDA

Hello, I left a message earlier. This is Gladdy Gold. Please call me."

I am very frustrated. Linda Silverstone is getting to be annoying.

Evvie opens my screen door, walks in, joins me in the kitchen. I notice she's still wearing dark colors. I can't get used to it. My Evvie, my Florida Parrot, a woman of many bright colors. She's in mourning and I don't know what to do to get her out of it.

"How are you feeling?" I ask.

She shrugs. She beelines to the stove and pours herself a cup of coffee.

"Want to do something today? Maybe a movie? I happened to notice, one of the local movies is giving out prizes at Wednesday matinees. Should I find out which theater?" Evvie keeps ignoring me. I press on. "Something you might want to review? People keep asking when they'll see another edition of your newsletter."

"Later. I don't know. I'll see."

"Listen, I need help. Give me some advice." Hoping I can get her interested in something, anything, I grab a cup, too, and sit next to her at my tiny dinette table.

The room is so undersized that just sitting down, we are nearly rubbing shoulders. When each of us first moved into our apartments, our description of the kitchens was that it was almost like living in a motor home. One person in here is comfortable. Two, we have to take turns moving and changing places. Three is a crowd and four's a mob scene.

"It's the new case. I'm trying to reach this woman who will not answer her phone. All I get is her machine. How do I make her talk to me? I've already learned she lives behind a locked gate. I know she won't open the door to a stranger."

Evvie, not terribly interested, tosses out, "When all else fails, try honesty. Leave her a message that explains what you want. And just keep phoning until she picks up."

Evvie glances at my last Sunday's crossword puzzle, which stays on my table until it's finished.

She picks up my pen and fills in one of the clues. "Nine down, 'state of pure pleasure,' is 'elated.' "

Suddenly, the word for me is elated, too. Evvie's actually showing a bit of animation. I look over her shoulder and take the pen and fill in another. "That gives me my across word. Thanks. And you know, what you just said is a good idea. I'm going to try it. We can take turns badgering her."

For a moment she hesitates, and then she smiles. "Include a turkey sandwich and you're on."

Without having to get up, I swivel around and open the fridge and take out sandwich stuff. Evvie gets up, walks three steps to the stove, and puts up another pot of coffee. I hold my breath. *Please don't let her change her mind.*

I pick up the cordless phone and dial again. Naturally, it's Dr. Silverstone's machine. While making her sandwich, Evvie nods her head, encouraging me.

"Linda, my name is Gladdy Gold. I am a private investigator. Your parents hired me to find out why you won't attend their anniversary party. They seem very concerned. Please pick up so we can talk. I will keep calling until you do. All I want is an answer and then I'll stop pestering you. Please." I wait, but nothing happens. Finally I hang up.

When Evvie finishes eating her sandwich she presses the redial button. "Hello, Linda, this is

Evvie Markowitz, Gladdy's partner. We're actually sisters. We're really very nice people, and part of our job is to help others solve their problems and be happy. Please pick up." She waits awhile, and then hangs up, too.

"Well done," I say. "But we're taking a big risk. This may really get her mad. She might just turn the machine off."

Evvie shrugs. "Maybe she will and maybe she won't."

Evvie, still sitting, digs in the fridge and finds last night's leftover peach pie. I am near tears of happiness. This is the first time she's shown any interest in eating. And I'm so glad I gave into gluttony and bought it. "À la mode?" I ask as I reach up over her to the freezer and whip out the vanilla ice cream.

She smiles. "You are so bad. Of course I want it."

I dial again. "Hi, Linda, this is the annoying Gladdy Gold again. I tried reading your book last night. I didn't understand a lot of it, but if we ever meet, I want to ask you—do your father's techniques really work? Isn't denial of an illness a cop-out? I'll hold, maybe you're in the bathroom and can't get to the phone quickly." After counting to ten, I hang up.

Evvie claps. "Great. Work on her ego. Maybe she'll get intrigued enough to answer your question."

"Think we should get the girls up here and let

them take turns? I'd love to hear how they'd talk to her."

Evvie, always the actress, says, "Don't bother; I can play all their parts." She pretends to hold the phone to her ear. "Listen, you twerp, my name is Ida and just who do you think you are? Call me or else!"

I giggle. "Or else what?"

"I'll huff and puff 'til I blow your house down."

"Wait," I say, knocking my shoulder into hers as we giggle together. "Let me be Sophie." Now I pretend to dial. "Well hello, Linda. Just because you live in that great big house and you have expensive clothes, what makes you think you have any taste? Let me come and be your fashionista." I'm really getting into it now. Waving my arms, I say, "I'll give you fuchsias, and scarlet reds. Gold velvet—I'll make your house sing!"

A timid voice says, "Can I play me?"

We look up at the open kitchen window and the girls are standing there, watching us. They are not smiling. Though Bella is trying to be a good sport.

Evvie and I burst into laughter.

Within seconds they are inside.

Within seconds the room is filled to over-flowing.

"How long have you been listening?" I ask, hiccupping, as I try to stop laughing.

Evvie leans down, her arms on the table, her body shaking.

Sophie automatically opens the fridge and peers in.

Bella attempts to find a spot where she might stand.

Ida, half in the hallway, grabs the phone and presses the redial button. "If you're going to imitate me, at least do it right." She speaks into the receiver, her voice haughty and businesslike. "This is Ida Franz of the Gladdy Gold and Associates Detective Agency—"

Ida suddenly stops, in shock. "Someone's on the line!" As if it were on fire, she throws the phone at me while Evvie jumps up to press the speakerphone button on the phone base. Bella tries to move out of the way and at the same time Sophie tries to push past her to get out. Bella is knocked into the open fridge. Sophie tries to grab her as a box of cream cheese, a bag of bagels, and a carton of orange juice drop to the floor.

"Hello? Hello? Is someone there?"

While I'm trying to right the tumbling phone, I yell into the speaker, "Yes, this is Gladdy Gold. Are you Linda?"

The voice answers. "No, I'm her assistant, Marjory. Dr. Silverstone says you've made your point."

Evvie and I look at one another, chagrined.

"If you are available this afternoon at three

P.M. she will see you at her home. I assume you know where, that is if you are the owners of that very old, very dirty Chevy that was parked across the street all day yesterday."

"We'll be there," I say.

Evvie and I high-five one another. Bella and Sophie are busy putting the dropped things back in the fridge. Ida, arms crossed, legs akimbo, scowls at us. "You owe me big," she says ominously.

Evvie and I laugh again. And Ida joins in. "Gotcha!"

Bella, clutching a mayonnaise jar she can't find room for adds, "I don't think your car is that ugly."

23

LINDA'S SECRET

Linda Silverstone's assistant, Marjory, leads us through her massive house. Everything looks modern and expensive. And brand-new. Highly polished and spotless, as if no one ever touched any of the furnishings. It seemed as if it had been done by a decorator who intended it to look perfect forever.

Marjory's personal color scheme is dark and rigid. Black hair. Black-rimmed glasses. Black pantsuit and shoes. The only color, a red silk scarf. Her back is ramrod straight. Everything, including her prim expression, says no nonsense allowed here.

Bella and Sophie hold hands, oohing and ahhing at everything they see. Gaping up at the chandeliers. Sliding their shoes along the shiny mosaic entryway.

I am thrilled Evvie agreed to come along. Ida has mixed emotions, I suppose, now that Evvie seems to be back with us and Ida's no longer number one.

We travel down a long, elegantly carpeted hall to arrive at what must be Linda Silverstone's office. Wall-to-wall bookcases. Buttery leather chairs, each with its own Tiffany-style reading lamp. Lovely selections of artwork. I spot Linda's books displayed along a bottom shelf, next to a wall with her framed awards and degrees. All in all, a room to impress. Through the back windows I can see what must be a huge, elegant garden.

And finally, there is the elusive Linda seated behind her desk, a gorgeous French antique with gilt-edge trim. I wonder if it's an original.

Linda is what one would call a handsome woman. Not beautiful, but regal-looking, seeming younger than her sixty years. From the pictures in their books, she resembles her austere father.

We stand in the middle of the room, waiting for permission to sit. Or not.

"So you got your wish," Linda greets us sarcastically, her face held stiffly, her voice pinched and slow. "You may be sorry. Sit."

We quickly scramble for seats.

Marjory moves close to her side and attacks.

"You had no right to bother Dr. Silverstone with your ridiculous calls."

Ida is about to argue. I quickly squeeze her arm and whisper, "A little honey first, honey..."

I meet Linda's piercing look. "Please forgive us for the drastic methods, but you do make it difficult to make contact."

Linda whispers to Marjory. Marjory says, "Dr. Silverstone wants to know how much her father is paying you to spy on her. She says she'll double it for you to mind your own business."

Ida can't stand another second. "Hey, just who do you think you're talking to?"

By now I'm aware something is very wrong. Why isn't Linda speaking for herself? Evvie looks at me; I can tell she's thinking the same thing.

Marjory, the mouthpiece, charges, "I'm talking to five elderly busybodies who have no right to impinge upon her privacy."

Suddenly I realize Linda's head is quivering up and down and from side to side.

"Are you all right?" I ask.

"No, I am not all right!" Linda's voice is equally shaky; the words come out slowly and with great difficulty.

With that Linda is helped out from behind her desk. Marjory positions her behind a metal walker and places a tartan plaid blanket around her shoulders. We become aware that her entire body is moving convulsively. Marjory is about to speak again, but Linda stops her with a glance.

She is very hard to watch. Bella and Sophie want to turn away, but the expression on my face tells them not to. Ida and Evvie are as startled as I am.

Now I realize what it cost Linda to keep such control when we first walked in, but not any-more—she lets us have it, full blast.

Her body writhes, her face contorts, her head bobs every which way as she struggles to get the words out. "Not a pretty sight, is it, all these tics and tremors?"

For a moment, none of us speak. "May we ask what's wrong with you?" Evvie asks gently.

"Parkinson's."

Sophie gets excited. "Just like that actor, Michael J. Fox!"

Linda admits sadly, "Yes. Like him." She indicates to Marjory to speak.

"Linda's illness has progressively worsened this year. She no longer goes out in public."

My eyes tear up. "Your parents don't know, do they?"

She shakes her head with a spastic motion. "I don't want them to know."

"So that's why you refuse to go to their party?" Ida asks.

Now it's a shaky nod.

Marjory continues. "Now you understand why she cannot appear at a function where probably a hundred people will show up."

Sophie's voice is tentative. "But Michael J.

Fox is on TV and a million people can see him shake...."

To our shock, Linda starts to cry. Marjory reaches over and pats her shoulder.

For a long moment, none of us speak.

Linda indicates she wants to talk again. It takes a very long time for her to get all these words out but she is determined to explain. We have to concentrate hard to understand her.

"Do you know what it's like to have parents like mine? Health is their life's work. They hike ten miles a day. They are careful of every scrap of food they eat. My father does the Polar Bear Plunge in the ocean every January first. You were right on the phone when you said what they preach is denial. They do not like to face illness, and mine cannot be hidden anymore. I cannot deny it and make it go away. I will not be an embarrassment to them in front of everyone they know."

Bella and Sophie are tearing up. I'm having trouble staying dry, myself.

With Marjory's help, Linda gets herself back behind her desk once again to hide much of the shakiness. "My father will take one look at me and turn away in disgust."

Marjory steps forward, indicating it is time for us to leave. "Need I say, you will not mention anything you have seen or heard here to anyone? Especially to her parents."

I get up and face Linda squarely, then take a

deep breath. "When will you tell them, Linda? Or will you wait until you're dead and they can find out by reading the obits?"

Linda stares at me in rage. "How dare you ... ?"

Ida and Evvie jump up and move closer to my side to support me.

Linda, stuttering hard, can barely get the words out. She pounds impotently on her desk. "How can you be so cruel? Can you imagine what it will be like for them to have their only child die before they do? What it will do to them?"

"No," I answer her, "I can't, and I hope I never have to find out, but as a parent, I tell you it would be worse to not know when my child is ill. To not be able to be there for her. To not be able to help her through the hard time ahead." I pause for a moment. "I don't think you give your parents enough credit."

"Yeah," Ida says, "you'll be killing them along with you."

I look at Ida. Someday she is going to have to tell me the truth about what happened between her and her kids.

Evvie's voice is equally passionate. "They're all you have. Don't turn away from anyone who loves you. Give them the chance to show how they feel."

Linda bows her head. "And what if they fail me? What if *they* turn away?"

I walk to the desk and lean over toward her.

"Right now you believe you are all alone in the world. If they fail you, then you'll know you're right. But what if you're wrong?"

I reach out and touch her hands. "I am so sorry. Sorry for your illness and sorry we total strangers have invaded your home and been so hard on you. Forgive us. We won't bother you again."

I join the girls and we head for the door.

Evvie turns and says, "Good luck to you, Linda."

Marjory lets us out. She doesn't say a word.

We get into my car, but it's a while before I'm able to drive.

Ida reaches over so she can face me from the rear. She raises her eyebrows. " 'A little honey, honey?' "

Evvie defends me from her front seat. "Sometimes tough love works better."

I shake my head. "I shouldn't have done that; I had no right. But I kept thinking if one of my family were suffering like that, I'd have to know!"

"That poor girl," Bella says from the seat behind Evvie. "God help her."

No one says anything on the way home.

24

JERSEY JACK

Jack hopes he'll find Barbara Sutterfield sitting at a patio table at the rear of the Nabisco factory. The weather is still playing at Indian summer and it's pleasant outdoors. If he's wrong, he'll try the inside cafeteria. He hopes he won't have to do that. Then he might have to go through the rigmarole of the front office and state his business and the probability of being refused admittance. Maybe he'll get lucky back here.

He glances around, assessing what he sees, what he researched about the factory on Route 208. Basic bland nondescript cement building. Supports some nine hundred workers. Been around since 1958, and one of the three largest factories of its kind in the country.

There are fifteen or so people sitting outside,

taking their lunch break. They are in groups of two or more. He glances around and sure enough, there is one woman eating alone. If his hunch is right—that's his target.

Her head is leaned back, taking in the sun. Her feet are resting across a second chair. A half-eaten sandwich remains on a piece of Saran wrap. He assumes she's a chain smoker. There's a cigarette in her mouth right now, and a full ashtray. He studies her, waiting until she notices him. She looks about late forties, tall, too thin, long dark hair that seems like it doesn't get to a beauty salon much, if at all. She wears jeans and a T-shirt underneath her white lab coat. There's a weariness reflected in her body language. Her shoulders slump. Her hands hang loosely. Looks as if life hasn't been too good for Barbara Sutterfield, cousin of the elusive Patty Dennison, sole witness to the murder of Jack Gold.

What he's found out about her are two divorces and two young children ages four and eight, from different husbands. They're cared for by a next-door neighbor while she works. A dead-end kind of life.

When she sees Jack standing there, she drops her legs off the chair and narrows her eyes. Her shoulders stiffen. Like an animal sensing danger, she readies for attack.

Time to look menacing. Time to say hello.

"Barbara Sutterfield?"

She shoots him a sardonic smile. "As if you

didn't know." Her voice is hoarse from years of nicotine abuse. "You're the busy little beaver cop, asking too many questions all over town."

"That's me."

She grazes her eyes up and down his body. "Aren't you a little old to be playing cops and robbers?" She reminds Jack of wire fencing. Tough. Brittle. Unyielding.

People clammed up at the coffee shop, library, post office, grocery stores. What a tough town. What a tough broad.

"The case I'm on is pretty old, too."

"So I've heard. Ever heard the saying—let sleeping dogs lie?"

"It's a cliché and I don't believe in clichés. Especially when I'm trying to right a very old wrong." He moves closer. "May I sit down?"

She hesitates, and then she shrugs. He pulls over another chair and straddles it.

He sniffs the air. "It's really something the way you can smell the factory blocks away. I bet kids must love smelling chocolate cookies all over town."

"It gets old real fast. After a while the sweetness is sickening."

"May I ask what your job is inside?"

"Not that it's any of your business, I'm in quality control."

"Meaning?"

"I look at every single cookie and pick out the defective ones." She recites in a weary tone as if by rote. "Here's the twenty-five-cent tour. Every cookie formula is a secret. The dough is sent into a hopper, which feeds it into a machine that forms it into a strip. These strips are cut into shapes according to what kind of cookie it is. The whole mess is baked in an enormous walk-in oven. Cookies are cooled, and then decorated. Packaging is done automatically by machines that sort the cookies into bags for sale. We're open twenty-four/seven. Tour's over. Anything else you need to know?" She takes a last puff of her cigarette and glares at him disdainfully.

"Where's Patty Dennison?"

"My cousin's gone." She grinds out her cigarette and immediately lights up another. She makes no attempt to blow her smoke away from Jack.

"So I've been told. Over and over again. I'd almost believe it if everyone didn't say it like some old script they rehearsed. If I got an occasional 'I don't know' or 'Who?' instead of a universal 'Never heard of her,' maybe I'd fall for it. Amazing. I'll say one thing, people here are loyal."

"They should be. My family, what's left of it, which is me, goes way back to the beginnings of this town."

"So I've learned. A family who's worked for Nabisco as many generations as the factory's been here. You're the last of the line. You and your two kids."

She bristles. He's pressed the right button. Unnerve her now. Break the self-control. "You stay away from my kids!" She wraps up what's left of her sandwich and rises.

"Please sit down. I have no intention of interrogating your children."

Barbara sits back down, eyes narrowed, but on the edge of her chair, ready for flight.

"She's quite remarkable, Patty Dennison is. She's managed to live below the radar. No phone. No gas and electric bills. No voting record. No car. No known address. Quite remarkable in this high-speed day and age we live in."

"It's because she's not here anymore."

"So you keep saying. Then where does she live?"

"You don't listen too good. I said she's gone. Gone, like in dead!"

That stops him for a moment. His eyes laser deep into her eyes. "Where's her grave?"

"No grave. She was cremated."

"So, there'll be a death certificate on file, won't there?"

Her eyes twitch the way liars' eyes do. She hesitates a few seconds too long. "Yeah. Somewhere."

By now the lunch hour is over. Jack is aware of people standing up, tossing the remains of their lunches into the trash bins. He feels he will lose her soon. His intensity rises.

"Barbara, you are an intelligent woman, no

doubt about that. I commend your loyalty, but you're not a good liar. I know Patty is here. I can almost smell it by the way people avoid me. If she had died, people wouldn't be that jumpy when I confront them. You can make things easier for both of us by telling the truth."

He waits, but Barbara turns her face from him. She pretends to busy herself, sweeping crumbs off the table with her fingers.

"So be it. It will take more time, but I will find her. I'll go back to New York and use FBI computers that are so smart they could sniff out a flea on a moose in Alaska. Then I'll return."

Barbara tries to tough him out, but her drooped shoulders betray her. She cries out, anguished, "Leave it alone. It was forty-five bloody years ago. She's suffered and she died."

"Stick to your story, but there is a woman I love who has suffered as much or even more, not knowing what really happened to her husband that terrible New Year's Eve. So you can see I'm highly motivated to keep going until I find out what I want to know. Maybe Patty might find some peace if she faced me. Maybe she wouldn't have to keep hiding."

Jack gets up. He puts his hand gently on Barbara's shoulder. She flinches. "Please tell her that. I'll be at the motel until eleven tomorrow morning. I'm sure you know which one. If not, ask anybody in Fair Lawn."

He drops his card on the table. "This is my cell number. Call me anytime." He feels Barbara's eyes watching him leave, hears the flick of her lighter as she lights another cigarette. Hopefully, she'll pass his message on to Patty.

25

HERE'S THE DEAL

Here's the deal," I tell my girls. "There's only room in the limo for two more people. Of course I have to go, so who's joining me?"

"Limo," says Bella, letting the word roll over her tongue. "I like the sound of that."

We are sitting at our usual picnic table on the Lanai Gardens lawn where we sometimes hold our PI business meetings. I have just informed them that Linda Silverstone has decided to take our advice and face her parents after all. Quite a victory, I feel, because I took a big chance confronting her the way I did. Now I wonder if I should call her parents ahead of time and warn them of the shock that is coming their way. It took too much to get Linda's trust; I don't dare go behind her back. I am very conflicted. And nervous, too.

The sprinklers have only just shut off, so the grass is cool and damp under our feet. Nosy neighbors tend to stroll by, hoping to catch a bit of insider information even though they know we always clam up if anyone gets too close. But that doesn't stop them from trying.

The spying goes both ways. From our vantage point we can see Denny in his beloved garden, weeding happily. In a while Yolie will appear with drinks and sandwiches. He's teaching her English and she's trying to get him to learn a few words in Spanish. That little love affair is still moving along nicely.

And there goes Mary, getting in her car to take Irving to the hospital to visit Millie, even though she hardly recognizes him anymore. The gossip squad is watching this new twosome carefully. They are spending much too much time together and the squad is sniffing out impropriety. Mary and Irving better watch out.

"However, we have to leave for Naples around eight in the morning," I continue.

"I'm not too crazy about getting up that early," says Sophie as she polishes her nails. Today's shade is Passion Plum.

"And the trip will take about three and a half hours each way."

"A seven-hour round trip? Sounding less

thrilling, the more you tell us," comments Ida, crocheting as she listens.

Evvie is seated backward on the bench, leaning against the table, with her face lifted up to catch the sun's rays, seemingly not listening. Every so often, Ida looks over at her, checking for reactions. What's going on is this: Ida has been my assistant since Evvie has dropped into her depressive mood. Ida's waiting to see when she'll be replaced again, once Evvie snaps out of it.

"Yeah," agrees Sophie, "my tush would hate all that sitting, but the limo idea, I still like. Maybe they serve champagne in the car?"

I shrug. "We're meant to visit with the Silverstones and have a lovely luncheon prepared for us. As thanks for talking Linda into coming to their big celebration weekend, which starts the day after tomorrow. Linda wanted to do this before all the guests arrive Friday evening. Poor thing, she feels very negative about how they'll respond to her—"

Sophie interrupts. "I love the luncheon part."

I keep on. "...Then we head back home— assuming all goes well with the reunion of Linda and her parents. I'm sure they have a very impressive house. Naples is famous for having lots of rich folks living there."

Sophie sniffs. "Seen one mansion, seen 'em all."

"That's what I always say," says Sophie's shadow, Bella, our recording secretary, who is holding her notebook in case I say something worth recording.

Evvie wheels herself around and addresses me. "You haven't told them the good part yet. About the alligators and the Indians."

Now everyone is alert, staring at Evvie. I guess she's has been paying attention all along.

"What alligators?" Bella whispers, suddenly clutching Sophie's arm.

I try to nip this in the bud. "Come on, you've all lived in Florida for more than twenty-five years, and none of you have ever been on the west coast. There's a beautiful beach there."

Sophie snorts. "We have a beautiful beach here and we never go, so why should we ride in a car three hours to not go to a beach there?"

"How can there be a beach?" Bella wants to know. "The ocean is facing the wrong way."

"That's the Gulf of Mexico," Ida informs her.

"Mexico? Now we're going to Mexico?" Bella says, alarmed.

"Tell them that road is the only way we can get to the west coast, if one is driving." Evvie grins maliciously.

Now all eyes watch me suspiciously.

I sigh. Everything with these girls is always such a big deal. And Evvie is being a trouble-maker today. "The fastest way to cross this part of Florida," I say in my best travel guide voice, "is to take Interstate Seventy-five."

"Its nickname being Alligator Alley," says Evvie gleefully.

Naturally Bella and Sophie gasp.

Evvie adds, "It goes through the Everglades, which you all know is a swamp."

"Swamp!" says Sophie. "You want us to go in a swamp?"

Evvie says gleefully, "Filled with snakes along with the alligators. I did a travel article about it in my newsletter last year. I guess nobody reads anything but the garage sales and restaurant specials. This highway was the most fought-against road ever built in Florida. It goes through the Big Cypress Seminole Indian Reservation and has many nicknames: Killer Road, Suicide Lane, Death Row, the Road to Nowhere."

With that Bella actually jumps off the bench in horror.

"Evvie, stop it!" I tell her, really annoyed now. I try to reassure the girls. "It's a perfectly good highway; it's just boring with nothing to do or see. It's either that or fly."

"Okay," says Ida, recapping. "You want us to drive about a hundred and fifty miles for more than three hours each way on a very boring road that may or may not have snakes and alligators walking along it, just to have some lunch. And remind us why it's necessary to take this short, hard trip?"

"Because Linda Silverstone asked us to accompany her. I guess she wants some moral support for when she faces her parents with her illness. I promised I would."

There is a long silence at that. I sigh again. "Okay," I say without confidence. "Raise your hand if you want to join me on this trip."

More silence.

Swell.

"Thanks a lot. Evvie, since you are such an expert on I-Seventy-five, I elect you to be my traveling companion." I don't even bother to hide my sarcasm.

The girls applaud my choice. Even Ida is happy about letting Evvie take back her position of number one assistant on this. Evvie shoots me a dirty look.

"I'm sure we'll have a lot of fun," I tell her sweetly.

26

STRUCK OUT

Jack makes his early Thursday morning leave-taking obvious. He puts on a big show of paying his bill in the tiny front office of the motel and wondering aloud to passersby what the weather might be back in the city. He drops his duffel bag into his trunk. Stalling some more by going to the coffee shop across the road and ordering coffee to go, he lets everyone there know the cop is leaving town. He can almost feel their relief. Then he waits outside. And hopes.

Nothing.

He goes back to the motel and phones the Nabisco factory, only to find out Ms. Sutterfield has taken sick leave. No, no date when she is expected back. To Jack's surprise, for someone so secretive, she's listed in the phone book. But, then again, why wouldn't she be? She wasn't expecting the Ghost of Christmas Past to show up nearly fifty years later. When he sees her next, he'll remind her that there is no statute of limitations on murder.

On his way out of town he decides to pay her a home visit. Shabby street, shabby neighborhood. Barbara's conventional 1950s tract house is on a corner lot. House hasn't been painted in a very long while. Once it might have been a sea green, with a white trim; now the colors are faded and drab.

He knocks on her door. No answer. Not that he expected one. Clearly Barbara has run from Jack. He walks around the house to see if there is any activity in the rear. Shades all drawn. A kid's bike on the back porch. A few towels hanging on a clothesline. There's a doggy door. And a small food and water dish, with the name Spooky on it. Dog on sick leave, too?

Out of the corner of his eye he sees a window curtain next door being moved. He makes a calculated guess that this is the neighbor who baby-sits the kids. If he knocks on her door, she probably will pretend not to be home. But if it looks like he's snooping in Barbara's windows, she'll either come out in a huff or call the police.

Sure enough, as soon as he pretends to peer around the window shades, the woman comes rushing out her back door. Very foolish, the cop in him thinks. She's too gullible. A woman who can easily be taken advantage of. She should have called the police. She's in her sixties, white-haired, pudgy, wearing an apron with apple designs running along the border. Probably baking—face and hands look like they're covered with flour. She's a sweet motherly type. But right now, she's anything but friendly.

Hands on hips. "She's not home."

Jack shakes his head at her foolishness. He could be a burglar wanting the homeowner not to be home.

"She told me about you, that you'd be snooping around." She shakes her fist at him.

That explains it. Barbara warned her about him. Mother bear being protective of her cubs. No surprise, he gets the cold shoulder. Apparently Ms. Sutterfield has taken her children and dog away with on her "sick leave." And no, neighbor lady has no idea where she went or when she'll be back. So, just get away from here, she warns, or she'll call the police.

On his way home, driving the turnpike he phones Emily. No use putting it off. She's excited to hear his voice. She can hardly wait to hear what he has to tell her.

He doesn't want to drag out bad news. "Sorry, Emily. No luck."

He hears the disappointment in her voice. "Does that mean you're giving up?"

For a moment he has to concentrate when a Pabst beer truck swerves to get in front of him, narrowly missing a huge SUV merging from the other lane.

"Jack, are you still there?"

Recovering, he answers, "At this point, I don't know what else to do. My only lead left town. I scared Barbara off."

"Do you have to go back home to Florida right away?"

He thinks about that for a moment. "No, not really." Nothing much waiting for him there.

"Stay awhile longer. Maybe through the weekend. Barbara might change her mind and call you."

"I wouldn't take any bets on that."

"I'm sure Lisa will be glad to see more of you. My family, too."

What a lovely woman she is. "Perhaps I will. For a short time, anyway."

When he hangs up he feels better about it. He isn't ready to go home and have to face Gladdy and lie about his strange behavior. And know in his heart he failed her. He's happy to put off the inevitable. He's not looking forward to it.

27

DRIVE TIME

The trip is too quiet. Evvie and I are in the sleek black limo that Linda Silverstone has hired to drive us to Naples. For over an hour now, Linda has been stretched out across the three back seats, an afghan covering her, needing to sleep. Evvie is in no mood to talk to me. Last night we had quite a tiff; she insisted she would not go and I insisted she must. She can't understand why I didn't find an excuse to get out of this trip. What is the point? Linda will deal with her parents one way or another, and what are we supposed to do? I explained that her parents wouldn't take no for an answer. They insisted I accompany Linda and they want to thank me personally. Actually all of us were invited, but since

Linda hired this limo, there's only room for two more.

"Well," Evvie had said, "you should have gone by yourself if you don't know how to make people take no for an answer." I reminded her we were partners and I wanted her by my side. Impasse. We were both being spiteful.

So, this morning, still tired and annoyed, we are not speaking. Which is just as well, since anything we might discuss would have Marjory, sitting next to us, listening in, and the way things are between us these days, that's not a good idea. Evvie leans against the glass and stares out the tinted window, lost in her own thoughts. Marjory brought a book to read. And I'm sorry I didn't think to bring one also. As for the driver, he's closed the partition between us, so I can't find an excuse to talk to him.

I look over at Linda; even in her sleep, her body remains restless. Whether that's from her medical condition or a nightmare about facing her parents, I don't know.

I try making conversation with Marjory. I ask softly, "Have you ever been to her parents' house?"

Marjory just shakes her head and continues reading.

The three hours will feel like ten at this rate. I look out the window, too. Nothing much to see. Yes, swamps to the side of the highway. Then finally, one small store and gas station. I'm guessing we're about halfway there. I suppose the driver doesn't need to stop. I wouldn't mind getting out and stretching. He doesn't stop.

Evvie is determined not to speak to me, so finally, I close my eyes and start to nod off.

When my eyes open I see that Linda is awake and sitting up. Marjory is seated next to her and giving her some pills with water and then something hot to drink from a thermos. Evvie is discussing movies she has loved over the years. Linda, who admits she isn't much of a moviegoer, seems entertained anyway. Marjory maintains her stoic face.

"Well, look who's up, it's Sleeping Beauty," my devious sister says. "We're just about there."

Linda looks from me to her. "I'm so glad you both came along to help me through. I couldn't face this alone. Frankly, I'm terrified."

I give Evvie a look to say, *See, you meanie, I told you we should come along,* and her look back says, *I know, I'm sorry I was such a pill!*

I love that we can read one another's minds.

"What should I do? How should I handle it? What should I say?" When Linda gets agitated, it's even harder for her to speak clearly. She shifts in her seat, constantly squirming as she tries to hold a knee from swinging back and forth.

Evvie climbs back to sit on the other side of her. She takes Linda's shaking hand in hers. "Just be yourself. Let things just happen," she says.

Good for you, sister.

Linda asks, "But what if they look at me with revulsion? I won't be able to stand it."

"They won't, I promise you," Evvie says.

"You swear?" Linda says in an almost childish voice.

"I'd take odds on it."

Good old Evvie, always right there in a crisis.

"Me, too," I add.

Marjory takes a brush and brushes Linda's hair gently.

As she leans into her assistant, Linda says, "I just know I'll ruin their whole weekend. I should have planned to come afterward. How can I do this to them? Hello, Mom and Dad, here's your dying daughter."

Now Marjory gets upset. "Don't you keep saying that, Linda. You have an illness. You're being given the best of treatments. You don't know anything about the future other than that you're here now, and that's all that matters!"

Linda turns and hugs her. And Evvie and I watch, tearing up a bit.

"Now, let's get you looking beautiful," Marjory says, reaching into a purse and pulling out a lipstick.

The limo pulls into the circular driveway of a very large and gorgeous estate. The driveway takes us past rolling lawns and exquisite gardens. The house is reminiscent of the one Linda lives in, only larger. Linda sits with the three of us, all holding hands. I look at Linda. Her eyes are closed and I think she is praying.

The front door opens immediately as the limo pulls up. The Silverstones have obviously been watching for us through the windows.

There they are, just as they looked in the photos I've seen. Very healthy-looking, very agile, looking years younger than a couple in their nineties. Very tall, standing straight, arms around one another, big smiles.

I say a little prayer myself.

They look eagerly at the back door. The driver runs around to open it for us. Evvie and I get out first, smile and give little waves. We introduce ourselves. The Silverstones shake hands with us.

Marjory is out next and she walks with the limo driver to the trunk, where they remove Linda's metal walker. I watch the parents reacting to this unexpected happening.

The driver wheels it to the door of the limo as Marjory helps Linda out. With the driver's help, the two of them position her behind the walker as she holds on as best she can.

For a moment, nothing happens. It is a quiet tableau, our side watching the parents transitioning through a gamut of emotions as they see their convulsively shaking daughter.

Then, in moments, they are both beside her. They take each arm in support. Their questions fly; her answers are very slow. Like the doctors they are, the questions go quickly to the heart of the matter.

"What is it?"

She hesitates, hardly able to face them. "Parkinson's."

The parents gaze at one another for a moment, their silence speaking volumes. With remarkable control her father asks, "Who's treating you?"

"Phil Orloff at the Medical Center," she says, staring down at her shaking hands in theirs.

"Good man. Couldn't be better," her father says gruffly. "What are you taking?"

"Mirapex."

"Did you bring your medical records?"

"Yes, in my briefcase."

"Why didn't you tell us?" her mother finally asks, eyes watering.

"I didn't want to worry you."

"So you let us worry anyway, as to why our only child doesn't want to be with us?" Her father tries to sound strict, but his voice is faltering.

"I'm going to die."

I hear Evvie, beside me, gasp. I feel we are holding our breaths in the pause that follows.

Her father straightens and faces his daughter squarely. "So are we all, and God will let us know the time. We don't know and we shall not guess. We will enjoy whatever time we have."

Linda's father lifts her up out from behind the walker and into his arms. Mrs. Silverstone moves closer. Now their arms wrap about one another, hugging and crying. "You're with Momma and Poppa now and everything will be all right."

With that he carries Linda into the house, with Mrs. Silverstone at his side, holding her daughter's hand.

Marjory briskly takes a suitcase out of the limo and holds it alongside the walker, then wheels both inside. Tears run down her face.

The driver gets into the limo and parks the car in the nearby parking areas.

Evvie and I look at one another, standing alone near the open doorway. We are sobbing.

"You know what we need?" Evvie blubbers, clutching me.

"Yes, our families. We need our families."

"We have to go back up north. I want to go home and see my daughter, and my grandchildren," Evvie wails.

"Me, too," I wail back. "As soon as possible."

We pull ourselves together and enter the mansion to join the others for lunch.

28

WEDNESDAY,
JANUARY 3, 1962

GRIEF

Emily and her cousin Martha wanted to help, but their chatter was giving Gladdy a pounding headache. Martha kept asking questions about why they had to do these strange things to prepare for sitting shiva. Gladdy sighed. Twelve-year-old redheaded Martha not only looked like her mother, but she was so much like Evvie was at that age. Restless, impatient, highly excitable, and exhausting.

"Why do we have to shiva?" Martha asked, holding her hands tightly across her chest and pretending to be cold.

Gladdy answered her, "It's not about cold. 'Shiva' is Hebrew for seven; we have to mourn like this for seven days."

"That long?" Martha is not happy about this news.

"Are we religious, Mama?" Emily wanted to know. As sad as Emily was, she was caught up in the excitement of preparing to have guests come over.

Gladdy thought about what it would be like in a few days, when there would be no more visitors and everyone would go back to their lives and she and Emily would be totally alone. Then it would really hit her that her daddy would be gone forever. The truth about their future would bring the sorrow back. She told her, "No, not really," as she continued to line up every straight-backed chair she owned into a semicircle around the living room.

"Then why are we doing this?" asked Martha.

"It's our way of honoring our mother and father, your grandparents, who were religious."

"But why can't we wear shoes?" Martha continued.

Gladdy explained that the dark clothes they wore and the fact that they were shoeless was to show they were humbled by this sad occasion.

"What's 'humble'?" Martha insisted.

Evvie, who was covering all the mirrors in the house with sheets and towels, now stood on tiptoes to cover the one over the fireplace in the living room. She was careful not to dislodge the many photos of Jack set along the mantel.

"*Martha*," she called to her daughter, "stop being a pest and come help me."

Martha ran over to Evvie, to do her bidding.

Emily went to help her mother move chairs. "It's sad we don't have any grandparents like other kids have."

Martha commented, "Well, I have Grandma and Grandpa Markowitz."

Gladdy exchanged glances with her sister that spoke a thousand words. Joe's family was as good as having no family.

At that moment, Joe walked by, carrying a small basin of water on his way to the front door. He smiled at his daughter. "And you're very lucky to have them."

"Are they coming today?" Martha asked eagerly. Gladdy and Evvie knew why she was so enthusiastic. They always bought her love with expensive gifts on birthdays and holidays. Other than that, they were hardly around.

Evvie glanced at Joe, eyebrows raised. "Yes, Joe," she said, barely hiding her disgust, "when will they arrive to show their respect for Jack's passing?"

Joe mumbled, "You know how they are. They can't take depressing occasions."

"Yeah. I remember how they avoided the depressing occasion of our marriage."

Gladdy saw Martha lower her head as her parents sniped at one another. As if you could fool children. "Girls," Gladdy said to get them out of the room, "get the pillows, please."

They eagerly ran to do as she asked. Martha asked as they were heading for the hallway, "When can we eat? I'm starved. We haven't had a bite since yesterday." Martha was also a drama queen just like her mother. Gladdy glanced at her serious, unsmiling daughter. Emily was always the quieter one, letting her cousin be the leader. Emily had been crying all night, but she would be brave today for her mother's sake.

Evvie answered, "I told you we aren't allowed to cook. People will be coming soon and they'll bring delicious things for us."

By now Joe was out of their range of hearing. He was placing the water and washcloths outside Gladdy's front door so that mourners could respectfully wash before entering. He also left a small note telling people to just walk in. The door was left open.

Evvie raised her hands as if to stop her sister's words before she could say them. "I know, I know, no fighting in front of the kid. But sometimes I just want to wring his neck."

The girls came back with large bed pillows. Emily said, "I brought a big blanket to put under them, too, so the pillows wouldn't get dirty."

"Where should we put them?" Martha asked.

Gladdy smiled at the two girls trying so hard to be helpful. She felt the tears wanting to burst, but she managed to hold them back. "Along the wall, so when we sit, we can lean."

Joe came back into the living room, wiping his damp hands on his khaki pants. "Well, that's done. If you don't need me for anything else, I guess I'll leave you to it."

Evvie's eyes were slits. "Leave us to it!"

Gladdy grabbed Evvie's hands, to stop her from whatever she might do next.

Evvie took a deep breath and spit out, "I guess you're right. I don't need you for anything else."

He shot her a sharp glance, looking for the innuendo. She managed to keep a tight smile on her face, knowing Martha watched every movement of her parents' dance.

Their first visitor stood in the doorway. Joe quickly headed out of the room. "Come on, Martha, let's go."

Martha looked nervously from one parent to the other.

Evvie's voice was like ice. "Martha will stay here with her aunt and cousin, out of respect for her uncle Jack."

For a moment everything stopped, except for the innocent mourner who moved tentatively farther into the room.

Joe, furious now, turned and hurried out. Martha breathed a sigh of relief.

The neighbor, Mrs. Baroni, a rather shy woman from apartment 4B, stood where she was, uncertain.

"Mrs. Gold," Mrs. Baroni said, with what she thought was the proper funereal tone. "I'm so sorry for your loss. I brought you a little something."

Martha quickly grabbed the bowl. "I'll take it to the kitchen." Emily followed after her.

Gladdy and Evvie seated themselves on the floor on the pillows. "Thank you," Gladdy said.

Her neighbor looked confused as to where to sit. "Please," Evvie said, "use the chairs; you don't need to get down here."

Mrs. Baroni gratefully lowered herself down on a plain kitchen chair.

Gladdy thought about the reading she had done to prepare properly for this tradition, according to religious lore. It told her that the bereaved ones sat on the floor to represent having been struck down by grief. How true, struck down was just how she felt. She wondered if she'd be able to get through this day without screaming and tearing out her hair. Maybe that was allowed as well. She remembered photos of Indian women keening and throwing their bodies onto their husbands' caskets. If only she could do that, too.

She could hear Martha say from the kitchen, "It's just soup. I hate soup."

Mrs. Baroni looked chagrined. "I thought a little minestrone would be good."

Evvie reassured her. "Yes, it will be wonderful. Thank you again."

What are we supposed to do? Gladdy wondered. No one was comfortable. Maybe that was the point. The dead were gone, and the living should suffer in some way as well.

All she wanted to do was lock herself in her bedroom, hold tightly to Jack's pillow, and never stop crying. Instead she felt like a hostess at a bizarre party that no one wished to attend.

Mrs. Diamond, from the deli across the way, whose son had been in Jack's American Literature class last year, brought matzo ball soup.

Mrs. Gromsky from 6D, who used to sit on the stoop and tell Jack stories about her native Russia, brought borscht.

Mr. and Mrs. Hanrahan from 2B brought potato soup. Mr. Hanrahan reminisced about how Jack enjoyed his Irish jokes.

Mrs. Kim from the Chinese laundry around the corner, who did Jack's shirts with just the right amount of starch, brought wonton soup.

She could hear Martha whining in the kitchen. "Everything's soup. Where's the food?" It actually made her smile.

A group of professors and staff members arrived from Columbia bearing a huge gift basket. Maybe now Martha would find something she could eat.

The sight of their distraught faces almost released her hysteria, but Gladdy was determined to soldier on, to use that military forbearance.

Everyone had something wonderful to say

about her Jack. Bless them all, but please—go home; she needed to be left alone.

Some of them asked what she would do now.

Gladdy told them she'd probably go back to school and complete her Library Science degree.

Evvie looked at her, surprised. Gladdy had astounded herself. She hadn't given the future any thought. As far as she was concerned she had no future without Jack. But she knew reality would soon set in and she'd have to find a way to support herself and Emily.

The day finally ended. People had come in and out almost nonstop, including their own close friends, every one of them, a sharp reminder of how much Jack would be missed.

Gladdy and Evvie got up from the floor, stretching, their backs aching.

Their daughters were invited next door for pizza. They ran out, once they had permission. She heard Martha telling Emily that at last they'd get real food. Suddenly Gladdy heard them talking to someone in the hall. No more visitors, please, *she thought.*

Two policemen entered the living room looking properly somber.

"We're sorry about your loss," *one of them said.*

Gladdy thought she might scream if she heard those words one more time. "Why are you here?

Have you found the man who killed my husband?"

The taller, heavier one said, "No, m'am, nothing yet."

"Don't you dare give up, you hear me?" Gladdy couldn't take another minute of this.

"We won't. We came because we need a photo of your husband."

Evvie grabbed one off the mantel and handed it to them. "Please go, my sister needs to rest."

They nodded and left.

Gladdy stood there, staring at nothing. "They'll never find the killer, I know it."

Evvie put her arms around her. "We should eat something. Do you want soup or do you want soup?" She imitated Martha's pouting face.

"Let's have some soup," Gladdy said, managing a smile.

They ate the matzo ball soup in the kitchen lit with memorial candles. While trying to fit all the containers into the refrigerator, Evvie asked, "Did you mean it about going back to college so you could work as a librarian?"

"I guess. I'm going to have to do something. I might as well do what I've always wanted to do."

"We'll work it out. You go to school, get your degree, and get a library job. I'll take care of Emily." She held up the last bowl. There was no more room to fit it. "We have to eat this one now, we have no choice. How's minestrone go with matzo balls?"

Evvie gave Gladdy one of her special looks. Half smile, half grimace. Then they put their arms around one another. "It's just you and me and the kids, babe. We're all the family we've got."

With that, they both let go and sobbed.

29

TELLING THE GIRLS

We are in Murray's Deli having the early-bird special, which we almost missed due to the fact the limo didn't get us back from Naples until five o'clock. Evvie and I decided that breaking our news to the girls would be better served, pun intended, while eating out, something we all love to do. I may even offer to pay for dinner, for further softening of the unexpected turn of events we're going to throw at them. I have warned Evvie to wait until after everyone's eaten. Tact and full satisfied tummies will be needed here.

Okay, the brisket is on order (Ida), as are the boiled chicken (Bella), and stuffed cabbage (Sophie). Evvie is having the chicken fricassee, and all I want is a salad after that huge lunch we had at noon.

The girls are digging into the rye bread and the pickle and sauerkraut dish with gusto while they wait for the appetizers to arrive. Which will be followed by the soups and salads and then the main dish, and after that, the dessert, which everyone always wraps to take home. They are in a very good mood when it comes to going out for early birds. I hope they stay that way.

"So," says Sophie, "how did it go?"

"Very well," I tell them. "The parents were terrific."

Evvie adds, "They were thrilled Linda came and immediately confronted her illness as a family problem that they will all deal with together."

"Linda intends to sell her house and move to Naples," I add.

"All three Silverstones kept hugging us. We really did a mitzvah there." Evvie smiles proudly. "I'm glad I wanted to go."

Ida's eyebrows rise at that misrepresentation of the fact, but she doesn't comment.

Sophie says, "I'll bet you cried a bucket of tears."

"No kidding, Gladdy and I were in puddles. Which is why we have something to tell you."

I kick her under the table to remind her. First food!

Luckily here come the appetizers and no one pays attention to what she just said. All eyes are on their food. Pickled herring for Sophie, tomato juice for Bella, Ida has a half a grapefruit, and Evvie immediately digs into the chopped liver. I am losing my appetite altogether.

They happily eat away. I glance around. The deli is busy as always. Mostly women. A few families. A typical Thursday night.

In a corner, a group of happy Red Hatters. That's an idea that has been sweeping the country: retired women joined together to just have fun. Way to go, girls. More power to you!

Evvie, Miss Impatient, gives me a dirty look to mean, *What are waiting for? Let's get this over with*. My look back to her says, *Wait, or they'll lose their appetites*.

So, gossip and eating.

"Wanna hear something amazing?" Sophie said, forking another piece of herring, "Irving went into the pool today."

I stiffen. This is not good.

"He hasn't had a bathing suit on since Millie got sick five years ago," Ida comments.

"Was Mary there?" Evvie asks, on the same wavelength.

"Yeah," says Bella. "First time I've seen Irving sit in the sun. On a chaise next to Mary."

"Did anybody say anything? I mean after they left," Evvie asks.

Sophie pushes her plate away, and looks toward the waitress for what comes next. "No, but if you can read minds, they said plenty."

The soup and salad are next. This time Evvie kicks me under the table; I kick her back. By the time this meal is over we'll be black and blue.

"I wonder what the weather will be in New England next week?" Evvie casually asks into the air.

"Who cares?" says Sophie, pouring Thousand Island on her lettuce, cucumber, and tomato salad.

I shoot Evvie a look: *Cut it out*. Evvie ignores me.

"Well, it is fall and the autumn leaves will be tumbling down. So pretty to see the colors of the leaves." Evvie pretends interest in peppering her tomato soup.

"So you want falling from trees, go look at the palm fronds on the ground tomorrow," suggests Bella.

Evvie daintily wipes her lips. "I rather had in mind taking long walks in the woods with my daughter."

Ida is now sniffing that something is up as she sees the glances between us. "Neat trick, considering your Martha is in Connecticut." She looks at me. "And you're thinking of long walks in Central Park with your Emily?"

"Can't pull the wool over Ida's eyes." Evvie manages a phony smile.

"What's up? Out with it," Ida insists.

All eyes are on Evvie. The plates are taken

away and now the main dishes are placed in front of us.

"Well," says Evvie lazily, "Gladdy and I decided to go up north and visit our kinfolk. We need a family fix."

"Really?" says Bella. "When are you thinking of going?"

"Saturday," announces Evvie.

"Which Saturday?" Sophie asks, alarmed.

"This Saturday." Evvie starts eating her fricassee.

Bella drops her napkin. "That's the day after tomorrow."

Evvie is delighted with herself. "We actually called on our cell phone in the limo on the way back home and made the reservations."

Just as I was afraid, interest in eating has palled.

Forks lie untouched as the girls turn to me, since I haven't said one word yet. I try for damage control. "We won't be gone long." I feel terrible. I don't know what to say to make this any easier on them. Evvie just couldn't wait, could she?

"What about us?" Bella says, her head bowed.

Sophie adds, "What are we supposed to do while you're gone?"

Ida crosses her arms, and narrows her eyes. "We had plans."

At last Evvie realizes her tactics were wrong. "Hey, come on girls, you can't be without us one teensy-weensy week? You got plenty to keep you busy."

"What about our tickets next Wednesday matinee to see that revival of *Fiddler on the Roof,* at the Broward Theater?" This from Sophie.

Evvie says, "Big deal, you can sell our tickets to someone. Besides, you've seen it ten times already."

"And what about the senior tea dance we were going to on Tuesday afternoon?" Bella is not happy.

"There'll be another dance...in a month," Evvie says, not daring to look at me.

"And the costume jewelry auction on Thursday?" Sophie jabs angrily at a spear of asparagus.

"You might have discussed it with us before you made all your arrangements." This from Ida through pursed lips as she pushes her plate away.

"You hurt our feelings," Bella says quietly.

"Hey, come on, you can't live without us?" Evvie tries laughing to lighten the mood.

Ida says, "Yes, we can do very well without you. You needn't worry."

Sophie says angrily, "You got that right!"

"Yeah, right," adds Bella.

Dinner is downhill from there. And the girls don't even wrap their desserts to take home. They just leave them there. Unheard of.

Afterward we drive home in silence. Everyone quickly gets out of the car and heads for their individual apartments. Evvie calls out, "Good night," but nobody answers.

"Glad?" She turns to me.

"I told you to wait until they finished dinner."

She is ashamed. "Bella was right, I hurt their feelings. Why am I so mean?"

"Maybe because you're hurting, too."

I give her a quick hug and head for my elevator.

"Evvie..." The voice seems to whisper out of the blackness of the night.

Evvie, about to open her apartment door, drops her keys, startled. "What... is someone there?"

"It's me, Joe." Her ex-husband shuffles toward her on the landing out of the shadows.

"You nimwit! You scared the hell out of me. Why are you lurking?"

He shrugs. "I was waiting for you to come home."

He picks up her house keys and hands them to her. She opens the door. "And what if we went to a movie or something and I didn't get back for two-three hours? You'd still be standing here like a schlemiel, dummy?"

She walks quickly inside.

He stands at the entry, his arms hanging loosely at his sides.

"Well, come on in, since you're here already."

Joe hesitates, and then walks in.

Evvie stands in the living room, hands on her hips, waiting. "Well?"

Joe looks around. "Nice place you got here."

"Really? I've only been here twenty-five years; you think you might have seen it before?"

"I was never invited."

"That's for sure. And you're not invited now, either. So speak your piece and go." Evvie stares bitterly at this man she lived with so unhappily for so many years, and then remembers Philip, the love of her life, who she'll never see again. Her eyes tear up. She sits down on the edge of her couch feeling shattered, thinking of life's ironies.

Evvie flicks at an imaginary bit of dust off her coffee table. Softer now she asks, "Why are you stalking me? Why did you move in here? What do you want?"

Joe continues to stand. "I don't want anything. Maybe to just be friends."

"A little late, wouldn't you say?"

He gives her a nervous grin. "Better late than never?"

She shrugs. "Not necessarily. Frankly, I have all the friends I need."

"Evvie, be reasonable." He plops down on the easy chair across from her.

Immediately she jumps up off the couch. "Hah, look who's talking. Mister I'm-always-right-and-you-never-are. Mister I-know-everything-and-you're-stupid."

"I'm sorry," he says softly.

She lifts her finger to one ear and turns her

head to that side. "What did you say? I can't hear you."

"I said I'm sorry."

"For what? For being a lousy husband and father? For treating me like dirt? That sorry?"

"Yes, I guess so."

"Too late." She walks to the door and holds it open for him.

He walks quickly to the door, angry now. "You're impossible. I can't talk to you!"

"Funny," Evvie says, "I used to say that to you all the time."

Joe storms out and Evvie shuts the door. For a moment she looks at the closed door, then leans her head against it and cries.

Twenty minutes later a secret meeting is held in the gazebo around the corner from Phase Three. No one is around. Everyone is either asleep or watching TV. Sophie, Bella, and Ida, wearing sweaters against the evening coolness, sit on the attached benches. Even the ducks in the pond are quiet. The only sound is of the evening sprinklers doing their nightly job of keeping the lawns alive.

"I'm mad," says Sophie.

"Me, too," parrots Bella.

"We are all in agreement," their leader of choice, Ida, tells them. "So what are we going to do about it?"

"Why can't we go to New York, too?" asks Sophie.

Ida answers her: "So who says we can't? We could take a vacation. Nobody will stop us."

"Nobody will even notice we're gone," Bella comments.

"That's for sure," says Sophie.

"We haven't taken a trip in years," says Ida. "Not since we went to Disney World fifteen years ago."

"If they can visit their folks in New York and Connecticut, so can we," says Bella.

Sophie gives her a gentle punch in the arm and reminds her, "You don't have any folks in New York, or anywhere else. You're an orphan."

"I forgot." She pouts, near tears.

Sophie and Ida both lean over to her and hug her. "We're your only family."

Bella sniffs and says to Sophie, "Well, you have family. We can stay with your son, Jerome, in Brooklyn."

"No, thank you," Sophie huffs. "When I got sick last month and you called him, did he bother to come down and see how I was? No, of course not; he was too busy. He's always too busy. I wouldn't waste our precious vacation up north to see him."

"Well," Bella says brightly to Ida, "what about your family?"

Ida reminds her that her family is in California,

but doesn't remind her that they are not on speaking terms.

"Okay," says Sophie, "we're on our own. Forget about family, think about fun. Where shall we go?"

Bella says, "How about the Statue of Liberty and Ellis Island?"

"Been there. Done that. Wore out the T-shirt." Sophie leans over and picks a gardenia from a bush right next to the gazebo. She sniffs it, enjoying its heady aroma.

Ida comments, "Yeah, about fifty years ago."

Bella adds, "So, it will be like new again. I was thinking we could visit our relatives there in the records they have on who came to America and when."

"Not a bad idea," says Sophie. "I vote to see a Broadway musical, maybe go dancing in Roseland."

"Sounds good," says Bella.

Sophie adds, "Maybe pick up some sailors in Times Square."

Ida and Bella stare at her.

Sophie grins. "Kidding...I was just remembering what I did when I was a teenager during the war."

"Okay," says Ida, summing up. "We'll make reservations in a nice hotel, cancel all our plans for next week, and pack and get ready for some fun in the Big Apple."

"And we won't even call Gladdy and Evvie when we're in the city," says Sophie.

Bella adds, "Not even once. Who needs them?"

The three girls slap one another's hands in a high five, then tiptoe back to their apartments and bed.

30

NEWS TRAVELS FAST

Hello, Emily darling." I love my new cell phone. I'm heading along the walkway to the laundry room and talking with one hand holding the phone and the other balancing my white plastic laundry basket against my hip.

"Mom, hi. How are you?"

"Just fine. Have some good news for you."

"Really? You're announcing your wedding? I already picked out my dress. I hope it'll match what you'll be wearing."

"Nice try, darling daughter. Keep the dress in a clean plastic bag, so it'll stay fresh. Guess who's coming to visit tomorrow?"

Emily sounds confused. "Visit? Where?"

"In New York. Your favorite mother is coming for a short trip."

Silence. I'm in the laundry room now and I quickly put my clothes in the washer, tossing my four quarters in to get it started. "Emily, are you still there?"

"Uh, sorry, Mom, I, uh, I dropped the phone. What a pleasant surprise." She pauses. "Any special occasion?"

"Something the matter? You sound strange." Like she's not happy at this news.

"No, just getting over a cold."

That's a lie. I can tell. "Does a mother need a reason? Well, as a matter of fact, we just finished up a case. And it made me realize how much I'm missing all of you. Still have that lumpy couch in the den?"

"Not to worry, you can have Erin and Elizabeth's room. But I warn you, you know what teenage clutter is like. I tried to get them to straighten up before they went back to college...."

"Nonsense, I was only teasing. The lumpy convertible couch is fine. So here's the plan. I get in late Saturday evening."

"We'll pick you up."

"No. Absolutely not. It's late. I'll grab a cab. And Sunday, all day, we can play. Okay?"

"Well, that's just wonderful. Can't wait to see you."

"Bye, sweetie. See you then." Am I imagining it? My daughter doesn't want me there. Nah, not possible.

* * *

Jack is making his way through the turnstile at Yankee Stadium when his cell rings. "Hello?"

"Hi, Dad. Lisa calling. I just had some interesting news."

"Oh, pregnant again?"

"Silly, no. I got a call from Emily. She just got a call from Gladdy. Gladdy is coming to New York."

"What? She's what!? Wait, hold on, I've got another call." Jack listens. "Hello?"

"Hi, Dad. Morrie, here. I had to call you. Guess what? I ran into Gladdy. She's heading to New York tomorrow night."

"Amazing. Your sister's on the other line, giving me the same news. Hold on ..."

"Lisa, that's your brother calling to tell me the same thing."

"Okay, Dad, talk to him, but call me later, we need to discuss how we're all going to handle it."

"All?" By now Jack is trying to find the aisle listed on his ticket. Throngs of people are trying to do the same thing, jostling him out of their way. The excitement of the crowd rises as it gets close to starting time.

"Yes, Emily and her gang and us. You're going to have to tell her you're in town. And that we all know one another."

Jack feels a decided chill. "I am? Hmmn, I see.

I'll call you later. Bye, Lisa." He switches back to Morrie.

"Dad, still there?"

"Yes, Morrie. Gladdy doesn't know I'm here, does she?"

"Believe me, she wasn't able to get it out of me, and it's gonna cost you big for that loyalty."

"What do you mean?"

"Never mind, I'll fill you in when you get home. Get this, Dad. I hear her phone's ringing off the hook these days, she and her 'assistants' are getting plenty of job offers. Your fiancée is really something."

"She's not my fiancée yet." Maybe never, he worries.

"Anything work out in Jersey?"

"Dead end, I'm afraid." Jack's mind conjures up the tense, chain-smoking cookie maker, Barbara Sutterfield, and how she shut him out.

"Sorry to hear that. But, Dad, don't give up. Maybe you'll catch a break, yet."

"Thanks, son."

"What are you going to tell Gladdy?"

"I don't have a clue." Literally and figuratively, he thinks, depressed.

"Gotta go. I wish you luck with Gladdy. You're gonna need it."

No kidding.

* * *

Jack hurries down the stadium steps to his seat on the first baseline where his pal Tim Reilly is waiting for him. He breathes in the crisp early evening air. Finally beginning to cool down. Ummn, wonderful.

"Hey, what took you so long? We're a couple a minutes from the national anthem. I got ya some dogs and watered-down beer. I'm already out fifty bucks."

Jack reaches into his pocket. "Let me pay."

Tim pushes his hand away. "How often do you get up here? Answer: Practically never. I can be a sport for a change."

"Thanks. What's a pennant race without dogs?" Jack looks around, taking in the capacity crowd at Yankee Stadium, anxiously waiting for the opening tilt of the crucial three-game weekend series. A sea of pinstripes waves before him. The fans are already screaming. He feels like a kid again, like when his dad took him to the Yankee games. Those were golden, wonderful days. With players who made history: DiMaggio, Mickey Mantle, the Babe ... A boy, his dad, and baseball—the American way of life, when times seemed less complicated.

In between bites, Jack comments, "All these free agents, who knows who's who anymore."

"And how lucky you were still in town and I could get another seat. It only cost me a couple a hundred bucks."

Jack quickly reaches in his pocket again, but

his pal Tim stops him once more, grinning. "Kidding. My pal Fisher couldn't come. Measles. Got it from his boy."

"Not that I deserve to be here. I said I wouldn't go to a game until I solved the case."

"I never held you to that. The odds were too much in my favor. So relax and enjoy."

They stand for the anthem.

As soon as they sit down, Tim says, "Now your girlfriend will never find out you were fried. It's a win-win situation."

"Yeah." More like lose-lose, Jack thinks.

Jack and Tim jump up again with the thousands of others as the Yanks come running from the dugout.

Jack feels fantastic. The years seemed to fall off. He's going to enjoy every minute. What's the line—eat, drink, and be merry, for tomorrow you die? Or something like that. He takes another big bite out of his ballpark dog.

It finally sinks in. *So Gladdy's coming in tomorrow. Now what do I do?* Never mind. It reminds him of one of Gladdy's favorite expressions, borrowed from Scarlett O'Hara: *I'll think about it tomorrow*. And that's what he intends to do.

First, let's play ball!

31

GLADDY IN NEW YORK

Evvie and I have a lot to talk about on the flight. Mostly about will we or won't we tell our daughters about our unhappy emotional state and the men who brought us grief. Our plan: Enjoy the kids and grandkids. Enjoy being back up north, where we grew up. Find fun things to do.

At the airport, we find the ground transportation area. I leave Evvie with the van driving her up to her daughter Martha's home in Westport, Connecticut.

The cabbie who is taking me into the city seems normal. At least I hope so. I smile, remembering cabdriver stories. New Yorkers collect these and treasure them to share at cocktail parties. One of my favorites was about the driver who went through a red light. I was a bit shaken when we missed a group of pedestrians by inches. When I pointed out his scofflaw behavior he made one of my never-to-be-forgotten comments of all time. Assuming I was a tourist, he said, "Listen, lady, in my town a red light is only a suggestion." I got out at the next suggestion.

Of course there were the crazies. I'll never forget driving over the Brooklyn Bridge in a blizzard with the driver who told me he was on antidepressants and described his dream; he would turn the wheel and go over the side of the bridge, and all his troubles would be over. I started babbling idiotically about how spring would soon be here and the flowers would be pretty and the sun would be shining, all the while clutching my door handle. *Don't let this be the night he acts out his dream.*

I realize I spoke too soon. I've got another Looney Tune. Here we are just turning off the Triboro Bridge and the driver pulls up to a curb and jumps out of the car, wielding a gun. In an accent I don't recognize, he says, "I be soon return." With that, he locks me in the car and starts running back toward the bridge.

Swell. I suppose I can get another cab, maybe. I can call 911 on my cell. I am sure getting attached to this cell. But the police will think I'm the crazy one. Locked in a taxi, with a cabbie toting a gun, running along the bridge? And besides, it's late, and I don't know how long I'd have to wait for another cab, and besides, I don't want to stand alone outside on a dark, empty street in a neighborhood I don't know. Forget all that; my luggage is in his locked trunk.

By the time I finish trying out my non-decisions, my vigilante cabbie gets back in, stows his weapon under his seat, and relocks the car. He turns around and, with a half-toothless smile that tells me he comes from a country with poor dental care, reports in whatever his accent is: "I a *politzia* in mine country. I see police chasing man on bridge. I go help arrest him."

My first thought is, Lucky the police didn't shoot this lunatic running toward them waving a gun.

My second thought is, If they did shoot him, he has the trunk keys and I'd be stuck in this taxi forever.

Welcome home.

My daughter's apartment is mostly dark. I let myself in with my own key. I assume Emily will be in the kitchen waiting up as she usually does when I come to visit. Some good gossip over *rugallah* and coffee! Light on, yes. But no Emily. There is a note telling me there is cold chicken in the fridge, if I'm hungry. They had a long day and had to get some sleep.

Welcome home?

*   *   *

I wake up to noises. The muffled sound of the coffee grinder whirring with something being held over it. Then the clatter of dishes and whispers of "Be quiet" and "Don't wake Grandma." One eye opens and I can't believe I'm seeing seven A.M. on the bedside clock. On Sunday? Are they crazy? I bury my head under the pillow and try to fall back to sleep, but finally, after fifteen minutes of twisting and tossing, curiosity gets the better of me.

Pulling on my robe, I stagger into the kitchen and voice my opinion. "On Sunday? Since when do you get up early on Sunday? Why is everyone up? Good morning."

I get a chorus of good mornings back. Then—

"Golf," says Alan, rushing by me sipping at his scalding coffee. "Gotta grab a sunny day while we still got 'em." And he is gone.

"Soccer," says Lindsay, looking adorable in her lavender uniform. She and brother Patrick are stuffing Pop-Tarts down their throats. "Our team is in second place! H'ray!"

"Skateboard for me," says Patrick, dressed like something from Mars in his huge black helmet, protective black-rimmed glasses, black knee and elbow pads, and all the rest of the paraphernalia.

Emily hands me a cup of coffee. "And guess who the designated driver is?"

That sounds familiar. "Wait a few minutes and I'll throw on some clothes and come with you."

"No time," Emily says. "Besides, I know you. When you come up to New York you always want a day to revisit your old haunts. So have fun. We'll see you later."

And the whirlwind whizzes by me with little cheek-pecks and lots of "Have fun"s and the kitchen is abruptly empty.

Huh? My night-owl daughter goes to bed early and my love-to-sleep-in-on-Sunday family are already out the door? And I want a day to myself? I told her Sunday was our play day. She didn't mention any previous plans. Oh, well, no use feeling sorry for myself. But I do.

I doctor my coffee the way I like it, toast one slice of wheat bread, sit down at their lovely oak table, and start to tackle the ten pounds or so of the Sunday *New York Times*. What bliss. Heaven.

Is this good parenting? Children and grandchildren so guilt-free, they leave Grandma to entertain herself? Or are they so used to being without me they don't need me at all? I always hoped my family would be independent, but this is ridiculous. Well, what should I expect? I call, give them one day's notice, and want them to change their already-made plans for me?

Well, yes. Actually.

Come on, I tell myself. *Finish your coffee and fold the paper 'til later. Time to hit the streets.* I'm so excited, I can hardly wait.

It's getting cooler, a little brisk, a harbinger of autumn in the air, but the sun *is* shining. It feels so pleasant after Florida's heat and humidity. Walking the streets of New York is one of the great joys in life. A thousand things to look at. A twenty-four-hour nonstop drama for your entertainment. Never boring. It's always risky for me to come here. I tend to go through the same shopping list each time and compare what the city offers and what Fort Lauderdale doesn't. Stimulation. And excitement. New York has everything. Fort Lauderdale? Well, it's a nice easy life, I guess. And I always ask myself the same question. Why am I there when I could be here? Never mind. I have places to go, things to see, and plenty to do.

First stop is always Zabar's. This world-class deli is the place closest to where Emily and Alan live. I turn off Eightieth Street onto Broadway and there it is. And it's the usual early Sunday morning chaos—the store is full as always, cars double-parked out front, lines around the block. The most amazing selection of food delicacies to be found anywhere. If there is a cheese somewhere in the world, you'll find it here. Or a fish, smoked or otherwise. Coffee, teas, incredible breads—you name it, they've got it. I walk in and let the smells engulf me. It reminds me of a sign I once saw in a deli. It read: "If I could live my life over, let me live it over a deli!" And this is the deli of all delis. A perfect way to begin my day. With a cheese Danish in hand I happily continue on my way.

Broadway, then Columbus Avenue eventually gets me to Lincoln Center, and I pay my homage to all the operas, the ballets, the concerts, I ever saw.

And then traveling a familiar path in Central Park, of course I walk awhile, recalling a hundred little memories—from necking on a bench with my first Jack when we were courting to wheeling Emily in her stroller, boat rides on the lakes, summer concerts, and on and on. A sudden pang of longing for Jack Langford hits me, wishing I could someday share all of this with him, but for the moment I am putting all of my Fort Lauderdale life out of my mind and focusing only on New York.

I head over to the real Broadway and all the wonderful plays I saw that shaped so much of my learning, honing my sensibilities, molding my life's philosophies.

When my feet start to ache, I hop on a bus. Later, for variety, the subway or a cab.

A short stop at the famous Forty-second Street Main Library where I used to work. It's closed Sundays, but I say hi to Patience and Fortitude, the celebrated pink marble lions, now faded gray, that guard the entrance to that beautiful, stately structure. Being as old as I am, I remember our famous Mayor La Guardia changing the names of the lions from Lord Astor and Lady Lennox (after the library's founders) to Patience and Fortitude to inspire us to muddle through the economic depression of the 1930s.

I stop for lunch. In the old days I would have gone to one of those wonderful Automats, but that grand old tradition is long gone.

Then hello to my alma mater, Hunter College, on Sixty-eighth Street. I dreamed of a picture-postcard Ivy League campus, but reality gave me a school to which I traveled by subway and received a vast and varied education. When I think of all the knowledge—schooling and experiential—that I've acquired in my life, stuffed in my brain, I wish there were some way to download all I know into some younger brain and save someone a hell of a lot of learning time. Who knows, maybe the computers will do that one day, too.

Onward. I have a very busy day ahead. And when I get home, that family of mine better be there to greet me.

32

THE GIRLS HIT NEW YORK

"Wake up. I'm dying for a cup of coffee."

Ida peers, through one half-closed eye, at her little travel clock on the plain brown-painted bedside table next to her matching brown-painted twin bed. She becomes aware of Sophie, leaning over in preposterous yellow Minnie Mouse pajamas, poking at her.

"It's only seven A.M. Are you nuts?" Ida shuts the eye and rolls over to the other side of the bed, puts the blanket over her head, and ignores Sophie. She mumbles, "I didn't dream you were a mouse; you really are wearing those pajamas."

Bella lifts her head up from the cot placed at the foot of both twin beds. "Is it time to get up?"

Ida mutters, "No, go back to sleep. We're on vacation here, remember?"

"But we didn't have any dinner last night," Sophie wails.

"Is it my fault the plane was late and we couldn't find an open restaurant when we got here? So much for the city that never sleeps." With both hands Ida pulls her pillow down over her head.

Frustrated, Sophie goes back to her bed, the other twin, and plops down.

Bella sits up on her cot, yawns and stretches. She is wearing a match to Sophie's mouse pajamas, only in pink. "I could use a cup of coffee, too," she says wistfully. She tries to get up, but flops back down, unable to get off the cot and onto the floor. Sophie comes over and helps her up. "Sleep well, sweetie pie?"

"Not very," says the martyr. "The cot is lumpy. But I don't mind as long as you girls got some rest."

"All right. All right. I'm up already." Ida, wearing white cotton thermals, jumps out of her bed. "Let's throw on some clothes and get a bite to eat."

With that, they are all in motion, not an easy job in the closet-sized room. Each one of them bends to the floor to riffle through her suitcase for an outfit. There is hardly space enough for the three of them to move.

"Where are we, anyway?" Sophie asks.

"We're in the Village, Greenwich Village,"

tour guide Ida informs them. "It should be fun down here."

"Right," says Sophie. "Besides we don't want to be uptown and accidentally run into Gladdy."

Ida shakes her head unbelievingly. "Yeah, there are only a few million people in the city; we wouldn't want that to happen."

After jockeying for turns in the bathroom and wiggling into their clothes, bumping into one another as they do, they finally leave their hotel room.

The streets are empty. No people anywhere. Sophie is musing. "Bagel and a schmear of cream cheese would be good."

"I'm thinking along the lines of scrambled eggs and onions with a kaiser roll," says Bella, licking her lips.

"Dream on, girls," Ida says. "I don't think we're going to find a Jewish deli in this neighborhood."

Ida points to a banner strung across from one side of the street to the other. It's held together from the top of opposite lampposts. It says, "LITTLE ITALY. WELCOME TO THE FEAST OF SAN GENNARO."

Bella wails, "But nothing is open."

"I guess we're up too early," Ida says with a tone that reprimands. "We could have slept another hour."

As they wander down the narrow cobblestone streets with their turn-of-the-century tenement buildings, they pass one closed store after another, one closed restaurant after another, a series of food carts on the sidewalks and in the gutters, each with huge signs hawking their covered wares: "MANGIA! MANGIA!" "GET YOUR ZEPPOLI HERE!" "EAT HERE! OUR CANNOLI IS THE BEST." "GET YOUR ITALIAN FLAGS HERE!" "GUCCI BAGS FOR SALE, $5.00! WE HAVE THE LARGEST SELECTION OF MADONNAS ANYWHERE."

Sophie's eyes are wide, Bella's mouth is open. Ida laughs. "You told me to pick someplace exotic."

"Oh, well." Sophie sighs. "When in Rome, eat...Roman."

Bella tugs at Sophie's sleeve. "Look, somebody else is here."

They glance over across the street to a huge, imposing church. On the bottom step an elderly woman dressed in black, shabby clothes dozes, her head leaning against the stone. Suddenly, to their surprise, the church door is flung open and a man comes running down the steps, both fists full of money. The old woman's eyes pop open and she jumps up screaming. "Thief! Thief, you rob the poor box!" She grabs at his leg to try to stop him. He easily shrugs her off. She screams in Italian, *"Aiutame! Aiutame!"*

He smacks her in the mouth. "Shut up, old fool!"

But she won't. He keeps hitting her, as she keeps screaming, banging her head against the wall.

Ida moves first. She starts running across the street, yelling at the top of her lungs. "Stop it! Leave her alone!"

Sophie and Bella are right on her heels. They are yelling "Help!" over and over again. The thief sees them and runs quickly around the corner. The girls can't possibly keep up with him.

They rush back to the woman, leaning over her, trying to help by wiping blood off her head, saying comforting words to her. Now others arrive, having heard the commotion. Someone shouts, "Call the police! Get an ambulance!"

An authoritative voice clamors, "Let me through, let me through." The owner of the voice is a large man, someone who obviously enjoys his food. His face seems chubby and jolly, though his eyes are hard, as if he's seen the shady side of life. A thin ring of grayish black hair circles his otherwise bald head. He wears an apron over his three-piece black, pin-striped suit.

"Philomena," he says, "are you all right?"

She reaches her hand out to him, and abruptly falls unconscious.

*   *   *

Over hot delicious cappuccinos and hard Italian rolls and butter, the girls are officially thanked for saving Philomena Pasquale's life by this man, who introduces himself. "I am Don Giovanni, father to all, of Mulberry Street. This is my Ristorante Firenze. We specialize in the best gnocchi in all of New York City and opera every evening at nine."

The girls look around and mumble their appreciation. The café is small, but intimate. The walls are hung with pastoral pictures of the old country. The tables are covered with brighter-than-white starched tablecloths. Each table has an empty round wine bottle tied with raffia string and a candle stuck in it. The Muzak is playing the theme from *The Godfather*.

Ida asks about the old lady. Don Giovanni shrugs. "Philomena Pasquale, eighty-eight years of age. She lives here in Little Italy all her life, since 1919."

Ida can't resist asking, "Why was she sleeping on the church steps? Is she a homeless person?"

Don Giovanni puffs his huge chest out. "Never! In Little Italy, we take care of our own. Philomena—how do you say it—she is a bit eccentric? Her whole family lives here, but in 1963, there is a big family fight and she moves out on them. She has anger of them all. She refuses to live with them, so she sleeps in front of the church in good weather and in the vestibule in bad. This is to shame them in front of everybody. The street provides her with blankets and much food."

Bella is impressed. "Since 1963? Wow! That must have been some fight."

The front door opens with a jingle of the overhead bell.

The police have arrived.

One is big and brawny, the other shorter but also brawny. They both have black hair and olive skin. They are both Italians and Don Giovanni knows them. Waiters rush over and immediately bring the cops tiny demitasse cups of espresso.

"So, what happened here, Don G?" asks the bigger one, whom Don G. refers to as Sal, as he takes dainty sips of his espresso.

"The poor-box robber finally hit our street. We watch for him day and night, but with the festival keeping us so busy, he caught us off guard. He finally hit our church and poor Philomena was in his way and he beat her up."

"No!" says Rocco, the other cop, crossing himself, shocked.

The Don nods. "She's at St. Vincent's. If it wasn't for these nice lady tourists here, she'd be at Pasquale's Funeral Home."

The girls perk up at the name. "That's her brother, Gino," the Don explains.

The two cops turn to the girls.

The one known as Rocco asks, "You get a good look at the perp?"

Sophie's shoulders go up proudly. "You bet we did! Right, girls?"

Ida and Bella nod in unison.

The little notebooks come out, poised to write.

Sophie says, "Tall, maybe six feet, maybe three hundred pounds, limps, wearing a baseball cap says Mets. But with black hair showing through the little hole in the back of the cap."

Rocco and Sal are impressed. "Nice detail," Sal says.

Bella pokes Sophie gently on her arm. "That's not what I saw."

Now all eyes are on her.

She explains in her usual whispery way. "He was a little heavy, but not much. He didn't limp; he just had a funny walk." She imitates Charlie Chaplin. "He had a backpack on his back. It had a picture of a skateboard on it."

They all stare at her in disbelief.

Ida's arms cross her chest. "Gladdy would be so ashamed. You aren't even close." She faces the three men with great assurance. "I got it right. Thin, maybe about twenty, dirty blond hair. *No hat*." She glares at the girls. "*No backpack*. What robbery were you watching?" Back to the cops: "Wearing jeans and sneakers."

There is a silence in the room. Don Giovanni throws up his hands in disgust. Rocco manages a smile. "Perhaps you ladies might come down to the station and look through mug shots? At your convenience, of course."

"Don't worry, we will," says Sophie, looking defiantly at Ida.

33

FAMILY PLOTS

Jack sits with folded arms, letting them all get it off their chests. His daughter, Lisa, keeps filling the coffee cups and the kids' paper cups of orange juice. They couldn't meet at Emily and Alan's place in case Gladdy came back early. Lisa was delighted to take her turn entertaining, giving Emily and Alan a chance to see where they live, only a few shorts blocks away. Their apartments are somewhat similar; buildings built before the war still had very large rooms with high ceilings and fine moldings. Whereas Emily and Alan's place was traditional in decor, Lisa and Dan had gone in for very modern furnishings. Both couples, however, wear the traditional Sunday stay-at-home-relaxing wear, jeans and cotton tops.

The two families are seated around the huge chrome and glass Berman dining room table, having a guilty brunch. Everyone has an aggravated point of view. All because of Jack.

"I can't believe I'm avoiding my own mother!" Emily moans. "We're stuffing ourselves here and I left her all alone on a Sunday morning to fend for herself. Do you know how weird that will seem to her?"

"Honey, what else can we do?" That from hubby Alan. "We're kind of in a holding pattern."

And the kids won't be left out. Patrick puts his two cents in. "And you can't even trust your own kids to keep a secret. We had to run out of the house like a bunch of chickens, wearing all our gear."

"Yeah!" Lindsay agrees with her brother. "We're not babies."

"I was afraid you'd slip," says Emily. "I didn't even ask about my aunt Evvie. Her own sister."

Jack's side of the family takes their turn, Lisa first: "Dad, don't just sit there. What should we do?"

His son-in-law the lawyer, Dan, reverts to logic. "I'm sure Jack has his reasons."

"I can't keep hiding from my mother," Emily says. "I have to talk to her sometime. What are you waiting for?"

"And what are you going to do?" Lisa's hands are on her hips defiantly.

"What are you going to tell her?" Alan asks curiously.

"And where?" Emily jumps in again.

"And how? Don't just sit there. Say something." Lisa, again.

All eyes turn to Jack. At the same time the kids, bored by their parents' problem-solving, leave the table as if by prearranged signal to do more fun things.

Jack throws his arms up in self-defense. "Hey, imagine *my* surprise. I'm about to go home and I learn Gladdy is coming here. This is a problem for me, as well. It has to be handled delicately. I'm almost tempted to leave and deal with it when she gets back."

"Oh, no, you don't. Then what do we do until she goes home? We have to pretend we never saw you?" Emily isn't about to let Jack off the hook.

"But, then again," Jack continues, "I think I'm better off talking to her up here without her girls getting into the act."

There's laughter from the Levinson family. They know the girls well.

"I honestly don't know how to handle this situation. I guess it might depend on how and where we meet. Imagine her surprise when I just pop up in front of her. And probably, shock. That will be a challenge enough."

Emily laughs. "You used to be a cop. You know how to deal with unsuspecting perps. Catch her off guard."

"Yeah, Dad," adds Lisa, chuckling, "make her do all the talking."

"Thanks a lot for your encouragement. Knowing Gladdy, I might get slapped. And I would deserve it for leaving her in the dark for so long." Jack stands up and stretches. "Too much good food, Lisa," he remarks to his daughter. "Telling Gladdy what I know will be the hardest part. After all these years to suddenly confront her husband's death again? I don't know how she'll handle it. And I've failed, so what's the point?"

Lisa says, "The point is you can't live with lies."

Emily nods. "Just be yourself, Jack."

He smiles at her. "Okay, here's a plan. Everybody have a cell phone?"

Patrick's voice rings out from the living room. Apparently the little scoundrels can play games and listen in as well. "Who doesn't own a cell? What a dopey question. You want my private number, too?"

Much laughter at that.

"All right. I'm not really stalling. Let's pick a time to get together for dinner at your house tomorrow night. I need time to think about how I'll handle this. I'll plan to meet Gladdy sometime tomorrow afternoon and explain everything."

There's silence at that. Then Dan says, "That's going to be a lot for her to absorb."

"I know. God help me. Emily, figure out where I should 'accidentally' bump into her."

"And after that shock, we throw a family dinner at her? Wow." Lisa stares at her dad.

"Hey, I'm looking for safety in numbers. At least I'll have all of you for protection when she starts beating me up."

There's smiling at that.

Jack continues. "I'll call right after I talk to her. I'll tell you what time we'll be heading for Emily and Alan's place. Give you, Lisa, and Dan, enough time to get over there. Is that plan enough?"

Long silence as the group absorb all he says.

Emily stands up, struggling to get into her jacket. "I know just the place for you to meet her."

Alan helps her get her arms in. "Now all we have to do is figure out how we get through tonight without one of us blabbing out the truth."

"There's only one way. We have to somehow never be alone with her. Oy."

34

NEIGHBORS

I wake up at five P.M. from my long, much needed nap to hear noise once again. Sounds like everyone's busy; everyone's moving about doing something or other.

I walk into the kitchen. "Hi, Mom, had a good day?" asks my daughter. She is efficiently unwrapping pizzas from their plastic wrappers.

"Fine," I say with a tad of sarcasm. "Visited all the old familiar places. And how was yours?"

"Hectic."

Alan walks in front of both of us, takes out paper plates from a drawer. "Good nap?"

"Excellent." What am I supposed to say? Convertible couch hard, nap bad, nightmares over the peculiar behavior of my family?

Patrick waves a DVD at me. "Grandma, seen this one? It's called *Eight Below*."

Lindsay always chimes in after him. "It's about dogs. And Antarctica. And they get left in a blizzard."

"Sounds exciting."

What follows is pillows being puffed in the living room and little portable tables being opened up and placed around the seating areas in the room. Lindsay brings paper napkins; Patrick is in charge of plastic forks. Alan fiddles around with the TV set and places the DVD in its compartment.

Emily removes a salad from the fridge and adds dressing.

"Can I help?" I ask. Am I a spoilsport for being disappointed with pizza and a movie, which seem to be the evening's plans? Yes. I am. Whatever happened to talking? Aren't they the least bit interested in me? Or more, about why I came to New York? They used to be thrilled to hear my tales from Florida.

"Nonsense, Mom, you're our guest," Emily says and pats my head as she passes me. Bringing the salad into the living room, she sets it on the coffee table.

Since when, I wonder. *This is new. I'm a guest?*

The doorbell rings. "Right on time," Alan chirps.

A couple with two children enter. The adults

carry covered dishes in their hands. After a flurry of greetings Emily turns to me and says brightly, "You remember the Wallers? Our neighbors, one floor down? Jean, Frank, Debbie, and Dougie?"

Maybe I met those people years ago, but I don't remember them. "Of course." I mimic all the cheery greetings going around. Obviously Debbie and Lindsay are great friends, as are Patrick and Dougie. The kids disappear immediately into the bedrooms, chatting away.

"Five minutes," Alan calls after them.

Emily explains. "This is a Sunday night tradition. Take-out dinner and a movie."

"How sweet," I say. First I've ever heard of it.

Emily shoots me a nervous kind of look as she brings the pizza out to join the salad and drinks on the coffee table. She is followed by Jean with her contributions of coleslaw, chips, and dips.

The men head for the fridge and do the "Let's get a couple of beers" thing, followed by a discussion of local politics. The women get right into recipes and PTA. I feel like I've landed in an off-the-air TV sitcom. Everybody Loves Everybody, so where is Raymond?

And within moments these young people, who move at the speed of a rocket shooting to the moon, are all seated at their little minitables with dinner in front of them. The kids come running, fill their plates, and grab seats on the floor. Alan puts the DVD on.

"Gladdy," Alan says, patting a space near him on the couch. "Have a seat."

And the barking sled-dog saga begins.

So I sit there, eat a piece of pizza, already too cool. Watch a movie, pretty good if you're into dogs and ice. Am I imagining it? No one in my family looks at me. Are they that engrossed in the evening's entertainment?

As soon as the movie is over, I excuse myself, saying I had a long, tiring day, and go to my bedroom, which is the tiny family den. The room is small but cozy. The art collection extends in here as well, but now we have prints, and photographs, all with a New York City theme. But that's only one wall, and includes the convertible couch. The other three have wall-to-wall built-in bookshelves, filled to the brim and indeed overflowing, not surprising from the daughter of a former librarian.

The tabletops have family photos. My favorite always has been the one taken in Central Park of my four grandchildren surrounding Grandma. The little ones, Patrick and Lindsay, are hugging me, but the teenagers, Erin and Elizabeth, are a bit more reserved. Naturally I love that one.

Once in my pajamas and robe, I pick up my cell phone and call Evvie in Westport.

"How was your ride to Connecticut?"

"Okay, nothing exciting. I napped."

"Mine was a bit dramatic. I had a cabdriver with a gun who thought he was Arnold Schwarzenegger."

"What? Something happened?"

"Long story for another time. It was actually an anecdote I was going to entertain my family with, but I haven't had a minute to tell them."

"Really?"

"I must be imagining it, but I think they are avoiding talking to me."

"That's weird."

"They're keeping something from me. I'm sure of it. My family is no longer my family. They've been replaced by something that grew in pea pods."

Evvie immediately responds, "*Invasion of the Body Snatchers*!"

"Right. I'll let you know when I suss it out."

"You know, I was going to say the same thing here. When I brought up the subject about Joe and why her father left their nice comfy setup to go live in Florida alone, Martha was very vague. And you know my talkative Martha, she's never vague about anything. I'll do some sussing, too."

"Keep me informed."

"Well, the heck with them. You're in the Big Apple, your favorite city; just go out and have a good time."

We hang up and I just sit there nonplussed. I

think about calling the girls. Or trying Jack, just to hear his voice on his machine. I ran into Morrie right before I left, and he still refused to tell me where his father was. Or maybe I should search the closets for the pods.

35

VILLAGE POLICE

It's no use," Ida says, leaving Rocco's office at the police station. "Besides, my eyes are crossing by now."

Bella and Sophie have already come out of the individual offices where the mug shot books were given to them to peruse. They are sitting on chairs waiting for Ida to rejoin them.

"Me, too, I'm dizzy," says Bella, leaning against the nearest desk.

Sophie has to agree. "Me, three. Either we missed him or he isn't in those books. Maybe he doesn't have a record yet."

They have been in the police station for over an hour. The thoughtful cop provided them with doughnuts and coffee, which they didn't refuse.

Rocco comes back. "You're fortunate, ladies;

pretty quiet for a Monday morning. All the week-end drunks are still sleeping it off. Sometimes it's a zoo in here."

Bella smiles. "I like zoos."

"Any luck?"

The girls shake their heads. Ida says, "No. Sorry."

They get up and stretch. Rocco leads them to the door.

Ida asks, "Do you happen to have a list of the neighborhood churches? With the names of the ones that were robbed?"

"We do."

"Could we have a copy?" Ida continues.

He looks surprised. "I suppose I can give it to you. It's public information. Any reason you want it?"

Ida gives him a big, toothy smile. "Oh, just a souvenir to take home to our friends about our exciting trip."

"Back home we're private eyes," Sophie informs him.

Ida punches her arm. Sophie punches back. "Shh," Ida says.

"Yeah," Rocco says, not listening. He leads them to the front door. "Well, ladies, at least you tried. You're good citizens. Now you can go back to the festival and have a fun day."

Outside Sophie says to Ida, "What did you punch me for?"

"Because we failed completely. I didn't want to

give the Gladdy Gold and Associates Detective Agency a bad name."

"So, what do we do now?" Bella asks.

Ida says, "Do what Rocco says. Let's have a good time." She grins at them. "And then figure out how to catch that crook."

The San Gennaro festival is in full blast. Crowds are everywhere along the cobblestone streets, having a good time. A forties-era band is playing on the bandstand and people are dancing the foxtrot. The girls, walking in the gutter, can hardly move. They are eating slices of pizza. With her free hand Bella is happily waving a small Italian flag. Ida scans the list Rocco gave them.

"It took us twenty minutes for this," Sophie says, indicating their treat. "Everything is one big line."

"And longer than that for the hot dogs. They were great." Bella smiles happily.

"They weren't hot dogs, they were Italian sausages," Sophie informs her. "And they weren't kosher."

"Who cares," says Bella. "They were delicious." She points. "What's this line for? It's really long. It's all around the corner."

"Who knows? Just get on. It must be for something good," Sophie says.

They join the end of the line. As they walk, each store they pass seems to have a loudspeaker blaring music. One is playing Sinatra, another is Julius La Rosa, another plays Perry Como. The girls wiggle their way along the line.

Ida indicates the list of churches. "Well, Saint this and Saint that...St. Joseph's Church on Waverly Place was robbed. And St. George's Ukrainian, too. According to what I pulled from the yellow pages, that leaves four churches that weren't hit yet. The closest ones to us are St. Veronica's and St. Luke's of the Field. I say we try one of them." She is suddenly aware she's in a moving line. "What are we getting this time?"

"Who knows?" says Bella. "It's so far away, it'll be a surprise."

Ida glances up and down the line. "Mostly women. Wearing black."

"Maybe it's the five-dollar Gucci bags. To go with the black outfits," Bella explains.

"Never mind," says Sophie, "Pay attention. Let's make a choice. Which church should we stake out? Gimme the list." She takes it from Ida and reads. "Hey, get this. According to our guidebook, St. Luke's is right next to Sophia's Restaurant. That's gotta be a sign."

"Okay, St. Luke's it is," says Ida. "When?"

They pass a small group playing a game on a little strip of dirt down an alleyway. The sign reads: "PLAY BOCCE!"

"Can we stop?" Bella asks.

"No, we'll lose our place."

Bella is disappointed. "I like bowling."

A few minutes later, they pass a man with a huge scale. "I can guess your weight," shouts the hawker. "Only three dollars. Your money back if I'm wrong."

"This I gotta do," says Sophie.

"Why?" asks Bella, annoyed. "You didn't let me stop to play ball."

"Just hold my place." Sophie rushes over to the obese guy in a green, red, and white striped suit who is running the scale concession.

Suddenly the line forges ahead. Bella calls, "Get back here, we're moving."

They turn the corner from Canal Street back onto Mulberry. From around the street they just left, Bella and Ida hear loud voices. Sophie is shouting, "You guessed wrong! Gimme my money back."

The man is yelling back at her, "You wiggled around on the scale. Stop jumping up and down!"

"I want my money back!"

"No, get lost!"

"Maybe you oughta get on your own scale. You'll break it and be out of business!"

Huffing and puffing, Sophie turns the corner and rejoins them. Bella asks, "Did you get your money back?"

"Of course I did." She is pensive. "Maybe I did gain a little weight. Maybe I should return his money."

"Let's get our minds on business," Ida says. "We're doing St. Luke's. What day?"

Bella says, "Well, tomorrow is Tuesday and that's seven letters. Seven is a lucky number."

All nod. "Okay, St. Luke's tomorrow, Tuesday. Time?"

Sophie mentions that three is her lucky number. "Three P.M.?"

"But that's broad daylight. Would he take that chance?" Ida asks.

"My lucky number says so," says Sophie.

"Works for me," says Bella as she nods her approval.

They now see their line approaching a church with a sign saying, "MOST PRECIOUS BLOOD CHURCH. WELCOME."

Suddenly they are aware that the line travels up the steps to an open door and that one by one, the people are entering the church.

"I think this is a mistake," Ida says "Quick, let's jump off."

But they are already too close to the front of the line. Sophie shrugs.

In the inner vestibule there is a priest standing near a sign that reads, "HOLY MASS. NOW IN PROGRESS."

They watch as each woman crosses herself, then the priest places something on their tongues.

When it's their turn, Bella curtsies.

*   *   *

"Well, that was interesting," Sophie says as they make their way back down the steps. They analyze the "cookie" they just ate.

"Could have used a little sugar," says Bella.

"I would have preferred chocolate," says Ida. "The wine was good."

"I would have liked seconds." Sophie shrugs. "Oh, well, never look a free cookie in the mouth."

36

SHOPPING

The Salvation Army is a treasure. The girls have a ball trying on the weirdest things they can find, looking in the mirror and giggling. They don't care if the other shoppers stare at them in annoyance.

Bella holds up a witch's black hat and a broom. "This is cute."

"Wrong holiday." Ida finally says, "Enough with the fun. If we're going to pretend we're bag ladies, we have to find some scruffy-looking stuff. We'll meet in the dressing room in ten minutes."

It isn't really a dressing room but three brown cloth-covered screens and a mirror. Ida and Bella are helping one another combine a series of ragged items into an outfit of sorts. They use ratty-looking scarves and old shirts and long, loose skirts and old sneakers. The colors are either faded or dark and murky-looking. They are dressed in their "disguises" when Sophie walks in. "Ugh," she says at the sight of them. "I wouldn't be caught dead in *shmattes* like those."

"But that's the idea," says Bella. "We're supposed to be in rags, so the thief won't recognize us."

"Not me. Never." She shows them what she found. She holds up a lime green, off-the-shoulder evening gown with matching pointy shoes, clutch purse, and fake flower corsage with red and white flowers.

Ida is furious. "That's your idea of what a homeless woman would wear?"

Sophie presses the gown against her body and peers at herself in the mirror. She purses her lips, blows herself a kiss. "Gorgeous," she says.

Bella is confused. "I don't get it."

"My role will be that of a drunken, drugged-out heiress sleeping it off on the church steps. Maybe we'll pick up a cheap bottle of champagne for a prop."

Ida looks at her, this impossible roommate, fairly stuttering with indignation. "You...you... are *not* a team player!"

Happily carrying their purchases, the girls exit the store. Ida says, "Now all we have to do is find a hardware store and buy our props."

"I've got the list." Bella reads off: "Fly swatter, bug spray, rolling pin, whistle, toilet plunger—"

Suddenly Sophie interrupts her by pinching Bella excitedly.

"Ouch. What?" Bella says in pain.

"That was him! That guy across the street."

"What guy?" Ida asks. "I see three women."

Sophie is jumping up and down. "It's the thief. He just ran around that corner. I would know that face anywhere!"

With that, balancing her shopping bags as best she can, she runs after him.

"Wait for us, for heaven's sakes," says Ida.

Bella hobbles after them, falling steadily behind.

Sophie and Ida turn the corner. This street is fairly crowded.

"Where is he?" Ida asks.

Sophie points. "There. The guy in black. Let's grab him!"

"Hold your horses," shouts Ida.

By now Bella makes her way around the corner, puffing and wheezing, stopping to lean on a lamppost to catch her breath.

Sophie charges through the shoppers on this busy main street like a bowling ball heading down the lane for a strike.

"Gotcha!" she screeches, dropping her bags and grabbing onto the man's shoulders.

As she pulls him around, Ida catches up with her.

The startled man stares at his assailants in surprise. Both Ida and Sophie see the round white collar at the neck of this all-black outfit at the same time. "May I be of service?" he asks, trying to make sense of the attack. "I'm Father Francis Xavier. Who might you be?"

Sophie slumps.

"Who might she be?" Ida says malevolently. "She might be a card-carrying lunatic!" Ida pulls Sophie away by the scruff of her neck as a small crowd gathers.

"Sorry," mumbles Sophie, backing off, her face turning red.

Ida pulls her across the street to where Bella is standing, watching fearfully. Sophie shrugs off Ida's hands. "He's a dead ringer, I tell you. The spitting image!"

Ida shoots her an exasperated look. "Not even close. That was the priest who gave us the cookie; that's why he looked familiar."

As they stand there, Bella looks at Sophie and Ida and asks, "I wonder what Gladdy is doing? I hope she's having as much fun as we are."

37

GLADDY AND JACK
AT LAST

Cell phone-itus.

Busy Monday morning at the Levinsons' once again. Dr. Dan off to Einstein Hospital. Kids to school and Emily meeting a friend at the gym. Which I wasn't invited to join. So New York City, here I come again.

I can't believe I'm walking down a Manhattan street with my phone glued to my ear. And as I look around me, just about everyone else is doing the same thing. How chic can I be? The streets are full, as always. The pace is fast. The city buzzes with excitement, as if important things are happening every minute. Construction continues to block the streets as newer and newer buildings go up to replace or redo the old. Even the venerable, world-famous old Plaza Hotel, after a hundred years or so, is getting an overhaul—or rather, what they call a "conversion." Along with the hotel, they're advertising condo suites for sale starting at $1.5 million!

I can't decide what to do next. I've already done MoMA—the Museum of Modern Art, which had a great retrospective of Picasso—so now the Guggenheim or the Jewish Museum.

I can't resist—I buy a salt-laden pretzel, no mustard, from a vendor on Sixty-fourth Street and munch happily for a few blocks. Finished, yum, licking the salt off my hand. My cell phone rings.

"Hi, Mom. It's me, Emily. Just checking to find out when you're planning to come home."

Interesting; first I'm ignored and now she wants a rundown of my activities. "Well, I was going to hit a few more museums."

"Good, but before you head for home, could you do me a favor?"

"Sure, name it."

"Well, we're having a few people in for dinner. . . ."

Again? More people around so they won't have to talk to me? I've got to nip this in the bud and have a little chat with my social-butterfly daughter. "You know, Em, I'm getting a little tired. I think I'll skip the museums and just take a nice long walk home. What do you need?"

"Could you stop at Zabar's and pick up a few things?"

"You said the magic word. Can't think of anything I'd rather do. Any excuse to drop in there. What do you need?"

"Three seedless ryes and an assortment of cold cuts. Pastrami, salami, corned beef. About a pound each. You choose. You know what we like. And don't forget the coleslaw and potato salad. Lots of it. And let them deliver it; too much for you to carry."

"My pleasure. And I'll pick up some halvah for the kids."

"Great, see you soon. Oh, and Mom, sorry we haven't had much time to talk. Maybe later tonight."

Hmmm, a little sensitivity at last. But I intend to chat sooner. "That sounds like a good idea. I'm on my way. See you."

Things are warming up at the old homestead. It's about time. I think about this list. How many people is she expecting? That's a lot of food.

Jack's cell phone rings. He's been waiting for Emily's call standing outside of a coffee shop near Broadway at Seventy-seventh, where he's been drinking too much coffee as he paces and worries. He's actually sweating. Gladdy's gonna kill me, he thinks. I know it. And I deserve it. He answers the phone.

"Hi, Jack. It's Emily."

"I figured. It's time, huh."

"Yes. She's on her way to Zabar's now. Figure she has about a fifteen-minute walk. If she speed-walks."

"My guess is she'll stroll and enjoy the sights. Don't worry. I'll be there before her. So, all systems go. Call the others."

"Will do."

He turns and heads uptown. He has plenty of time. Or not enough time, before the ax falls. On his head.

The cell rings again. It's Morrie. "Hi, Dad, how's it going? Talked to Gladdy yet?"

He groans. "Don't sound so gleeful. I'm about to walk into the lion's den."

"I'll be reading the New York *Daily News* online tomorrow."

"Why?"

"To find out how she murdered you." With that Morrie cackles.

"Very funny."

"Good luck, Dad. You'll need it."

And still laughing, he hangs up.

Zabar's. Huge and mobbed as always. Jack doesn't need to hide. She'll never see him until he reveals himself. He stands next to the international fish department; the incredible smells of smoked salmon and herring torment him with pleasure. He's reworking his opening remark when he spots Gladdy entering the store. He waits a few moments, so she won't see him, then picks up her trail. But, surprise! He's lost her already in this crowd.

After a few minutes of dashing from department to department in this warren of little rooms, he finally spots her standing in line in the cold cuts section. Here goes nothing. Or rather here goes everything. For a moment, he stops to look at her. She is so lovely. He hadn't realized how much he missed her.

On an impulse, Jack gets in the line, standing two people behind her. He doesn't know why, maybe just to stay close. He's relieved the woman in front of him is so large. He hopes that when Gladdy swings at him the large lady could be a buffer. He keeps stepping to one side, glancing around in front of the woman.

Two more customers and it'll be her turn. He removes his sweaty Yankees baseball cap and mops his forehead.

One more. Why are the clerks so fast today when he wants them to be slow and hold off his pain? What's going on? Usually buyers have a list a mile long, and they take forever in major discussions over every little purchase. He can't believe it—one quick item and done?

Gladdy's turn. She asks for a pound each of pastrami and salami.

"Don't forget the corned beef. That's my favorite," he calls, leaning in front of the large woman. The woman looks at him, annoyed.

Gladdy doesn't hear him. He tries again, louder. "And a pound of corned beef."

Now Jack pulls ahead of the woman and directly behind Gladdy. He says even louder, "Hey, Gladdy, I'm just mad about corned beef."

The woman glares at him. "No cutting in."

Gladdy stiffens and turns slowly.

Jack's voice wavers but he continues on. "Tell him to make it lean."

She sees him, just as the large woman pushes Jack sideways away from her. Gladdy's face registers her shock.

"Jack?" She grabs onto the countertop to steady herself.

He tries to move up to her, but the large woman grabs him by the scruff of his neck and shoves him back. "I said, no cutting in!"

"You aren't going to faint, are you?" he calls out to Gladdy as he is being forced backward.

"Good riddance," the woman says. People in the line clap. They close ranks in case he tries to get in front of them. Jack is jostled even farther back.

Gladdy can't move. Now the woman turns on her. "Finish your order or get off the line."

Gladdy hurries to where Jack is standing. Jack makes his move. It's do or die. He grabs her and kisses her, hard. He holds her tight enough so she can't pull away. She isn't trying to pull away. Thank God.

The crowd turns from booing to clapping. This is no usurper; this is romance. Romance is good. Everything in New York is free theater.

We are standing outside in front of the store. I am still in shock. Stupidly I say, "I didn't get the cold cuts."

Jack smiles. "Forget it; she's making pot roast. It was a ploy."

"A ploy?"

"Yes, to get you here so I could meet up with you."

I'm trying to make sense of this. "My daughter, Emily, told me to come here."

"Yes, she did."

"You know that? You know Emily?"

He looks sheepish. "Yes, I do. I have a lot to tell you."

"I would certainly think so." I keep my voice very steady. "I don't know how to react. "Have you been in New York all this time?"

"Yes."

"Why?"

"It's a very long story. Shall we find a place to sit and talk?"

I am still reeling. "But I'm expected home."

"No, you're not. Not yet."

Jack looks at me deeply, his eyes sparkling.

What the hell is going on? I don't even know what to feel. Am I furious? Or so glad to see him? But I know two things for sure: I'm damned curious and I feel my legs tremble and about to buckle under me. He grabs my arms and holds me tightly.

38

WONDER OF WONDERS

We are in yet another coffee shop down the street. Jack sits opposite me across the Formica table. He stares into my eyes as if he wants to drown in them. I see and feel such love from him. People must be walking back and forth, but I am no longer aware of anything but the man in front of me and the sound of his voice. I still can't believe he's here.

Wait a minute. I'm angry at him. This better be good.

"Why didn't you tell me where you were going?"

"At first because I was sore at you and yes, even jealous, because you were putting the girls before me."

"That's silly."

"Probably. I did a lot of thinking about our relationship. And then I decided I had to find a gift for you to truly show how much I love you."

I am starting to melt, but I'll be damned if I'll show it. "You could have just said so."

"Not enough. Not for me or for you. Not for our future together."

I need to think about what he's saying. But not now. "So running away to New York was an answer?"

"I hoped it would be. But I'm a coward. If I failed, I wanted you never to know I was here or what I attempted."

I'm confused. What could he mean by that?

"Brace yourself, honey. This is going to be hard to hear. I came to New York to find out who killed your husband."

I gasp. My heart starts pounding. What is he talking about? I pull my hands away. He waits, I assume, for me to absorb this bombshell. I can barely speak. I whisper, "And did you find out?"

"No, not yet. But I may be close."

I sit, stunned.

"Do you want coffee? Water? A gun?" He grins.

"Nothing. Just talk."

I shake inside as he tells me about his search for Patty Dennison. How he discovered she had lied and had hidden the truth all these years. How he met a reporter named Milt Paxton, who found her in a small town in New Jersey, but lost the trail.

He went into detail about going to her hometown and meeting her cousin Barbara, who knows where she is and won't tell him. But he isn't done with Barbara yet. He will get it out of her.

It is taking him a long time, but I feel as if I cannot breathe. I can only listen and feel. The tears become sobs. I am vaguely aware of people glancing over and quickly turning away. I cannot stand to listen one moment longer. I can't. I turn away toward the window.

He is standing outside, looking at the menu in the window. He wears a gray rain jacket and gray rain hat. It is raining.

But it isn't raining.

Noises are gone. I no longer hear the dishes rattling around me. No one in the coffee shop is moving. They are all stopped in their tracks, except for Jack who seems farther away. His lips are moving, but I no longer hear him.

Nor do I hear the traffic noises. The waiters stop taking orders from the tables. They, too, are motionless. Like the game of Red Light, Green Light we played as children. Everyone is frozen in time.

The man outside in the raincoat smiles at me. I squint to see his face. I can't see him clearly, but I know who it is. Oh, God, I know. The rain falls, hard.

"Order the cheesecake," he says. He smiles.

"Only if they have blueberry," I answer.

Family joke. He always ate the blueberries out of my pie.

"It's nice his name is Jack, too. So even if you call out my name by mistake he'll never know." He laughs as if he is enjoying himself.

"Stop that. I'll never forget you, my beloved husband."

"Time you did."

"Why is it raining when it isn't?"

He shrugs. "Maybe where I am it is."

"My darling. I miss you so."

"Think of what he's trying to do for you. What a marvelous act of love. He's trying to free you."

"I don't want to be free."

"It's enough! It's time you moved on."

He begins to fade as the rain lessens.

"Wait. Where are you going?"

"To the past, where I belong."

"Gladdy. Gladdy!" Jack moves over to the chair next to me. He shakes me. "Where did you go?"

I am barraged by the noises. The dishes, the conversations, the traffic.

I quickly look to the window. The sun is shining. People walk briskly along to the thousands of places that city people go. My dead husband is no longer standing there talking to me. What an imagination.

"Isn't it a beautiful day?" I say.

"You seemed like you went far away."

"I'm here now."

I take a last look out the window. A young woman holding a puppy in her arms glances at the menu.

I wave at her.

She smiles and takes the puppy's paw and waves back.

I get up. "Let's go home, darling."

39

TWO FAMILIES

Jack warns me I'm about to be surprised. But he won't tell me anything else. He waits until I can sort of put my face back together again in the tiny ladies' room of the coffee shop. I do the best I can, but my eyes are still red. We walk slowly, arm in arm, to my daughter and son-in-law's apartment. I'm aware that he doesn't ask directions; he knows the way. I ask him more questions, deeper questions about what he found out about Patty Dennison. I crave every little detail. The town she lives in. What people think about her. What they say about her. More about her cousin. There is such a huge vacuum I need to fill.

And finally, when I have heard enough on that subject, I try to tell Jack about Evvie and how torn apart she is over how her love affair ended. Apparently Morrie has been filling him in all along.

"Poor Morrie. I gave him such a hard time."

Jack laughs. He knows that, too. "Don't worry. He's a big boy. Maybe it will teach him a little humility."

We arrive at the apartment building. I hold tightly to his jacket.

"Here we go," he says, almost too brightly.

"What else should I know before we go upstairs that you haven't already told me? Don't you want to tell me how you know my daughter?"

"All will be revealed," he says in his best mysterious voice.

I use my key to open the door. At first I can't see anything. The lights are off. "Oh, no." Have they gone out again?

Suddenly all the lights are turned on. And a crowd stands in the living room, grinning at me. I look, trying to figure it out. Emily, Alan, Patrick, and Lindsay are on one side, and oh, my God, my granddaughters are home from college, my oldest ones, Elizabeth and Erin. All standing there with goofy smiles on their faces.

On the other side are...strangers. Don't tell me they've invited more neighbors...?

Jack points. "Allow me to introduce my family:

Lisa, Dan, Jeremy, and Jeffrey, and in the cradle, Molly."

I turn to Jack, astonished. "They all know one another?"

Emily confirms it. "Jack introduced us."

"We met at Back to School night," Patrick contributes.

I punch Jack's arm as hard as I can. I am furious. "You did all this without my being here or even knowing about it?"

Lindsay yells, "I told you she'd be mad."

Jack puts his arms over his face and head, protecting himself as best he can. "Help!"

I punch him again and again. "You don't tell me where you're going and I worry myself sick about where you could be! And here you all are having family gatherings without me!"

"I warned you, Jack," Emily says.

I shoot my daughter a dirty look. "Cold cuts, huh?"

She grins and shrugs.

"Go get him," Lindsay cheers her grandma on.

"Yeah." Patrick jumps up and down. Jeffrey and Jeremy begin jumping with him.

Erin and Elizabeth run over to me, crushing me with big hugs. "What are you doing home?" I ask. "School's not out."

"We didn't want to miss the fun." This from Erin.

Her sister agrees. "Any excuse to take off a couple of days."

Jack moves slightly away. "Thanks for saving me, girls." He bows. "Delighted to meet you."

I glower. "I'm not finished with you, yet."

I keep shaking my head. I can't believe it. My heart is so full, I can hardly stand it. Lisa comes over and hugs me. She is so beautiful. Her husband, Dan, gives me a shy hug, too.

"Champagne," Alan announces as he begins pouring. Jack hands me a full glass.

Emily raises her glass. "To my incredible mom, Gladdy."

"To Grandma!" All the kids raise their cups of apple cider.

"To Gladdy," the adults chorus.

"To wonderful you." Jack kisses me. In front of everybody. There's no getting out of this. Ever. I'm sunk.

There's a happy flurry of good-byes. Lots of hugging and kissing from Jack's lovely family. The kids' raucous, though sleepy, "See ya"s. In the background Emily and Alan are already clearing the table of the dessert dishes.

Then there are just the two of us in the foyer. "What an incredible evening," I say, holding Jack close.

"The best," he says, nuzzling my hair.

Then it comes to me. Now what? I'm here. He's here. What do we do now? We are now officially a couple in the eyes of these two traditional families. I'm sure the women are already planning engagement showers and invitations, the whole shebang. The men, making golf dates together. Heavens, even the kids from both families are melding. Especially young Jeremy, already mad about adorable Lindsay.

Well, I came here to be with *family*; now I've got them in spades!

But how do I feel? What do I want to do right now? What happens now?

As usual Jack reads my mind. He kisses me gently on my forehead. "This has been some emotional roller-coaster day for you."

"To put it mildly."

"You need to get a good night's rest." He smirks.

Yes, it's a smirk and I know what he's thinking. Then he actually says it to me.

"Right now I'd like to tear our clothes off and have us do amazing acrobatic things to one another. Depending on what our old bodies can do."

I look at him, astonished.

Then he laughs. "Meet me tomorrow for breakfast. Nine A.M.? Meet me in the lobby of the Dartford Hotel." He hands me a card with the address. "We have a lot to discuss. And to plan."

After one more kiss, this one quite passionate, Jack leaves.

I return to the living room where Emily is

vacuuming. She grins at me. "Must have been four pounds of potato chips I just vacuumed up. Remind me to never buy them again when all these kids get together."

I flop down on the couch. "You amaze me, all of you. All this plotting and I never catch on. I'm suspicious as hell, but I never get it."

"How could you have imagined this?"

She turns off the machine and she sits next to me on the couch, too, kicking her shoes off as she does.

"I couldn't." I smile. "All of you running out early on a Sunday morning to get away from me? I should have known. You all hate getting up early on Sunday. You usually stay in all day reading the *Times*."

"Guilty." Emily moves closer to me and leans on my shoulder.

"Sunday night pizza and a movie with the neighbors? A tradition? Still, dummy me doesn't catch on."

"They *are* good friends, and they jumped at the idea of being in on a secret."

I lean over and kiss her. "You're the greatest. Loony, but wonderful."

"About Jack..."

"Yes," I say, leery now. "What about him?"

"Well, if you need my approval, you've got it. He's quite a guy."

"He is, isn't he?"

"So, what are you doing here?"

For a moment I don't get it, but then I do. I pull myself straight up on the couch. I feel myself blushing. "Emily!" I don't know what else to say.

Emily gets up, yawns, and stretches. "I'm exhausted and off to bed. You know what you look and sound like? Me, at fifteen. See you when I see you."

With that, she walks out on me, grinning and chuckling.

I sit there, stunned. My daughter assumes Jack and I have been to bed together.

How can I tell her that, because of my indecisiveness, we haven't? If I tell my daughter, who is now behaving like the parent instead of the child, how I mucked up Pago Pago, she'll laugh herself silly.

40

GLADDY AND JACK
TEAM UP

Need I say what I went through in the morning? I looked through the few clothes I brought for family visiting: nothing dressy or, dare I say it, sexy? Not that I have too many articles of clothing under that category. I do the best I can with a pale blue cotton skirt and blouse and dark blue sweater. And a very plain pair of beige sandals. Jack is waiting for me and I am dressed to go out and meet him for breakfast.

I'm still reeling over what a turn of events occurred yesterday. Never in a million years could I have guessed it. What I wanted to do last night was call Evvie in Westport, but it was so late when we turned in, I couldn't make the call. Later, when I have a minute.

I grab a quick cup of coffee in the kitchen, and

this is what I get: Emily flashes me an enigmatic smile. Obviously she and Alan exchanged some choice pillow talk last night. Alan looks at me slyly, then quickly buries his head in the morning *Times*.

"Grandma, what are you doing here!" This from my tousle-haired, nineteen-year-old Erin with the sleep-encrusted eyes.

I look stern. "Where am I supposed to be?" I pray she doesn't answer.

She giggles and goes back to pouring soy milk over her granola.

I'm glad Elizabeth's still sleeping or there would be another country heard from.

Thank goodness eleven-year-old Lindsay is clueless. Or else not quite awake yet. Her nose is in a textbook. "Shh," she says, "I've got a test today and I need quiet."

"Well, you always leave it to the last minute," Erin snipes.

"How can I study any sooner? All we do around here is party, party, party." Lindsay snaps her book shut and, with a haughty shake of her head, takes it with her down the hallway to her room.

I could swear she's muttering something like "Old people don't do sex anyway."

Not so clueless after all. I hear Alan chuckling behind his newspaper.

That does it. "Well, I'm off. See you later."

As I am about to shut the door behind me I hear Emily call, "Don't hurry. On our account."

I groan. Families!

We have breakfast in a small restaurant down the corner from Jack's hotel. Jack informs me his hotel's coffee shop is toxic and to be avoided at all costs.

I can't help it; I'm beaming at him—and yes, there's a glimmer in his eye.

"I won't tell you what my family put me through with their innuendos."

"I can guess. Lisa called me at dawn to babble about last night."

"Dawn, really?"

"Well, it seemed like it."

The waiter brings us scrambled eggs and bagels. We dig in. I'm starved. I could hardly eat a bite last night.

"What's your choice, dear Glad? Business or pleasure first?"

I pause. This is a trick question. "Care to describe either?"

"No." He slathers cream cheese on his onion bagel. He's having a good time.

"Too much cholesterol," I say to stall.

"Yes, I know," as he smears even more on. "All right, a clue. Both will be very intense. Bad intense and good intense."

I sigh. And laugh ironically to myself. Since I

have a good idea of what he's up to, I don't know which terrifies me more.

I answer him: "Perhaps the business first. Then the pleasure can be like . . . dessert?"

He reaches over and takes my hand. "You need to be brave about both."

I manage a smile. "Brave? That's what I'm afraid of."

"Business first, then. We'll get through it, together."

I brace myself and he begins.

"I was just about to go back to Florida when I heard you were coming. I was ready to give up my quest to find Patty Dennison. I got close, but I failed. It's truly remarkable in this technological age that she is off the radar. There is no information to be had about her anywhere. When I met her cousin, Barbara, I was sure I would get her to tell me where she is. But she kept insisting Patty was dead. I almost believed her at that point. Then she ran away from me. At first I thought it was because I scared her and she didn't want to deal with the past. But maybe she ran because she was lying and she was afraid I could break her down. I'm not so sure either way. Regardless, I can't stand the idea that I failed you."

Now I'm the one reaching for his hands to comfort him. "Why don't we try again?"

"We?"

"Yes, we."

"Can you handle it?"

"I don't know but I guess I've always needed to learn the truth."

We stare into one another's eyes. I feel his strength. He is trying to judge mine.

The waiter brings us more coffee.

"I've called Barbara so many times, but she never answers the phone; I get the damn machine. We could go up to Fair Lawn, but she can get a restraining order and I don't put it past her."

"Funny you should say that, because the girls and I just finished a case where a woman refused to take our calls. We finally got her to answer."

He smiles. "Leave it to you and the girls. What did you do, nag her until she went nuts?"

"Pretty close. We just kept calling and told her we would not stop."

With that, Jack whips out his cell phone and hits a number. Jack listens. He shrugs. "Here comes the answering machine."

His tone gets stronger as he leaves her a message. "Barbara. This is Jack Langford. I am still waiting for your call. I will continue calling until you answer. I will call you at the factory as well and make things unpleasant for you there. I intend to come back to your town. You cannot avoid me forever." He leaves his number and hangs up.

"Well done," I say.

"Like spitting in the wind," he says, apparently not convinced this will work. He dials again. This time the Nabisco plant. "The operator is paging her," Jack tells me. "No answer. I'm sure she told them I'm some stalker."

"I doubt it," I say. "She wouldn't want police involved."

"Maybe she's still away. She took off with her kids like a shot after I confronted her."

The waiter brings us the check. Jack takes out his wallet.

"I'm guessing she's back. She needs her job. Probably she came back after she was sure you were gone."

"Now we wait."

"I have an idea. Let me call."

Jack looks alarmed. "I thought of that, but I didn't want to ask you."

"Jack, dear, from now on we're in this together."

"What will you say?"

"I'll say Gladdy Gold is calling and I insist on meeting with her cousin, Patty Dennison, immediately."

He hands me the phone.

41

SCENE OF THE CRIME

Jack and I stand in the middle of the street outside the coffee shop. The air feels good. The weather is starting to cool down. Indian summer is about to change into fall. People seem to be walking at a quicker, lighter pace. We glance at one another. I know what he is thinking. I know where he wants us to go. I want what he wants. His hotel is just up at the corner. But not yet. Something is making me hesitate.

"Up for a walk?" he asks, sensing my uncertainty. "We could window-shop along Fifth Avenue? Let's see if Rizzoli's bookstore is still there."

It hits me. "Jack, you'll think this is mad but I want to take you to my old neighborhood. Where it happened. Don't ask me why, but I need you to see it." I stare into his blue eyes. Like looking into pools of hot liquid. "The scene of the crime."

He checks my face to see if I really mean this. "Are you sure?"

"No. But something makes me want to do this. Maybe it's because I haven't been back there since I moved away two months after it happened. Maybe it's because we're doing what you came to do and this is part of it. Most of all, I can deal with it because I'll be with you."

He hugs me and then hails a cab.

"Our first taxi ride together in our first time in New York together," Jack says loudly as we make our way to the Upper West Side. Thank goodness we have a driver who's only playing hard rock on an ear-splitting wavelength. It could be worse. What really gets me is each time I've been in a New York City cab, the driver is talking on a cell phone at the same time. This one is, too. Madness.

I smile at Jack. How sweet. "Are you collecting anniversaries?" I shout.

We move very close together so we can hear one another, which is nice. "Sure. Why not?"

Bless him, he sees me tensing up the nearer I get to my old neighborhood and he's trying to ease it.

I try to concentrate on the nice things I remember of those earlier years. Being so near the Hudson River where I used to wheel baby Emily.

I'd sit on a bench and I'd enjoy the water views or read books as she slept in her carriage. And later, older, playing in Morningside Park. We pass the old markets where I shopped. Most of them have changed. And I remember how near Columbia University is to where we were. How much my Jack used to enjoy walking to work.

This Jack now takes my hand in his.

And we are here. In front of my old apartment building on 124th Street.

We get out. Everything seems to look the same. I notice the building now has a doorman. I lead Jack around the corner where our apartment faced the side street. I point to the window where I looked out and watched my husband every night when he came home from the university. Where Emily and I used to wave to him. The coffee shop on the corner is now a Starbucks. I slowly walk Jack down the alley. I haven't spoken a word, but it isn't necessary. His policeman eyes dart every which way, taking everything in. He sees what I see in my heart and soul.

Such a nondescript place for a man to die.

I bend down and touch the spot where so much of my husband's blood was shed. I think I can still see traces, but maybe it is just the accumulation of nearly fifty years of traffic. It all seems so benign in the bright sunlight.

We stand there for a while. I turn, slowly absorbing my old world. I hear birdsong, but I don't know which birds are singing. It reminds me of when a robin built her nest on our fire escape. Emily excitedly watched for hours, waiting for the babies to peek out of their eggs. There is the tinkle of a bell and a woman comes out of Starbucks sipping her drink. A couple of teens ride by on bicycles. I smell the cooking of many different cultures emanating from open windows above me. Of course my old curtains are long gone from my windows. Now there are drawn venetian blinds. Did the people who bought that apartment (I assume it is a co-op now) know of that tragic death on a New Year's Eve so long ago?

A wind suddenly whips around the block blowing leaves and bits of paper in miniature tornados. It always was a windy corner.

Or is it ghosts?

Jack stares at me with such kindness and understanding, I can hardly bear it.

"Enough?" he asks.

"Enough," I say.

42

THE DARTFORD HOTEL

As we are about to enter the lobby of the hotel that Jack is staying in, he says, "It's really old and shabby. Don't say I didn't warn you."

"How can I, Jack, dear, since you've already warned me at least ten times?" I give him a peck on the cheek. "I don't care."

In a panic, he starts to pull me away from the revolving door. "Let's go to the Carlisle or the Sheraton. There are a dozen hotels around here. Anything will be better than this."

"And what makes you think they'll have a room, last minute? And with no luggage? Can you imagine what they'll think? And what they'll charge?"

"I can't take you into this dump."

"Jack. Enough already. Let's go inside. I promise you I won't judge you by how dismal your hovel is." I smile sweetly, teasing him.

He gives in and we walk through the lobby. Walking is not quite accurate; he's dragging me to the elevator. He doesn't want to give me time to inspect its shabbiness. We hop in just before the door closes. There's another couple already inside. Typical tourists: three cameras around his neck, too many suitcases, still wearing shorts though the weather's changed, looking very small-town; harried. I smile at them. They smile back.

"First time in New York?" I ask.

They nod. They press the button for the twelfth floor, Jack presses the ten.

Just as we pass the ninth floor, I snuggle up to Jack, pretend to chew gum, and say in a Brooklyn accent, "I still don't know why they charged us full price if we're only using the room for an hour."

By the time everyone has had a chance to react and Jack turns beet red, the elevator doors open and I pull him out. "Welcome to the Big Apple," I call back to the shocked faces receding in the closing door.

I giggle. I can't believe the lightness I feel. Ever since we left my old neighborhood, something's changed in me. Something wonderful. I'll have to think about this later.

Jack is still stunned for a moment, and then he begins to laugh. "Gladdy Gold. I can't believe you did that."

"Hurry up," I say, "get me inside that cheap room, fast, before our time is up."

He pulls me along, shaking his head in amazement. "I'm shocked."

"Yeah, sure," I say, a huge smile still on my face. "I wish I could read the postcard they're gonna write from the big, bad city."

We get to the room. He pauses with the key in his hand. "I have something else to warn you about."

"Not another word. Just open it."

Jack opens the door and I enter.

He groans as I look around. I'm puzzled. "These decorations came with the room?"

Next to the window on a small table is one of those cheesy little statues of a hula dancer. I turn the switch and suddenly there are revolving colors and the hula girl is dancing to the "Hawaiian Wedding Song"!

On the bed are two matching colorful green muumuus, laid out next to one another. On the hotel pillows is a shiny white taffeta throw pillow with some kind of sea theme featuring sharks. The lampshades have plastic colored beads thrown over them. I stroll into the bathroom and there are matching shark towels.

When I walk back into the bedroom, Jack is

still standing at the door, stricken, as if by lightning.

"Don't say it. I know it's tacky."

"You did this decorating? To perhaps make up for the lack of decorating?"

He almost blushes. "I was trying to re-create Pago Pago. This was all I could find in one of those touristy T-shirt shops."

Ah, Pago Pago, I think wistfully. Our almost-perfect fantasy getaway. Stopped at a crucial moment of passion.

I peer suspiciously at him. "I have two questions. When did you find time to shop?"

He smiles, embarrassed. "Last night after I left you. A lot of these joints on Times Square stay open late."

"And how did you know I would come up to your hotel room?"

That stops him. He grins shyly. "I could only hope."

"It's adorable. You are adorable," I say as I pull him over to the bed and push him down onto it.

We tear off one another's clothes, piece by piece, rolling all over the bed, laughing and kissing as our passion builds. Wonderful, wonderful, wonderful . . .

And Jack's cell phone rings.

For a second we stop, startled. But then I keep kissing him madly, all over his face and neck. "Don't you dare answer that!"

"Don't worry, I won't," he says, nuzzling me and running his fingers through my hair. But he slows down.

Jack suddenly lets go of me. "Oh, God, what if it's Patty Dennison's cousin?"

"No, please no," I gasp, grabbing on to him again. "Don't pick up that phone! Remember what happened last time?"

"Just let me look at the caller ID."

As Jack crawls over to the night table where he left the phone, I hang on to his back and drag myself with him. Jack squints to read it. He obviously needs his reading glasses. I throw my arms around his neck.

"Damn," he says. "It is Barbara."

He pulls himself up to a sitting position, drops his legs to the carpet, and answers the phone. I throw myself back against the pillows, gasping for breath.

I hear him say, "Yes, Barbara, the two of us can make it by three. Yes, we'll meet you there."

He turns and looks at me as miserable as I am. "First we have to rent a car."

"First," I say, "I have to scream."

He leers at me. "We might have time for a quickie."

But we don't.

Why do I always think of my sister and movies she loved in times like these? Today's movie quote would come from the end of *Chinatown* when everything goes wrong and Nicholson's told, as if to explain why: It's Chinatown.

For us, it's Pago Pago.

43

STOP OR WE'LL SHOOT

No!" Ida and Bella both say in disgust. Sophie is voted down and she sulks.

"I don't know why you won't let me lie down on the steps and play the drunken rich lady."

"Because you look ridiculous," answers Ida. "Our perp wouldn't go near the church with something the likes of you lying there. Either he'll be blinded by all that greenness or burst out laughing and run away. And because you already made a fool of yourself, trying to capture that nice-looking priest who did not look one darn bit like the thief."

"Yeah," says Bella. "I should be on the steps."

Ida disagrees. "Bella, dear, you look suitably pathetic, but you'll get hurt. I'm stronger than you are, and besides, I'll get him with the rolling pin or the bug spray. Or Sophie will hit him with the toilet plunger. Then you can start whistling with your toy police whistle and wave your fly swatter."

This discussion takes place across the street from Sophia's Ristorante, next to St. Luke's, where the girls are hiding in the recesses of the doorway of a small quick-copy printing establishment with their chosen weapons.

"Well, we better decide because it's almost three o'clock," Bella says.

Ida shrugs. "The more I think about it, the more I'm sure this will be a waste of time. What are the odds he'll come to the place we chose? Especially in broad daylight."

The girls look around. There isn't a soul on the streets.

"We're already here," says Sophie spitefully. "So go ahead, Ida, you go lie down. I'll wait for you in the restaurant they named after me and get a bite to eat."

"Don't you dare," says Bella worriedly. "You see better than me. I need you to watch, too."

"All right," Sophie says grudgingly. "Besides, it looks likes it's closed until dinnertime." She glances out. "There's someone walking up to the church now. So I guess we better wait."

Ida peers out, then grabs Sophie's arm and punches her. "It's him! It's him!" She looks Sophie right in the eyes. "Exactly the way *I* described him."

"Where?" asks Bella. "I don't see anyone."

"He just walked into the church," says Sophie. Then, realizing it, "He just went into the church!"

Reality hits. The three of them jump up and down in excitement.

"Places, everyone!" Ida yells, as she rushes across the street.

"What places? I forgot," says Bella, turning around in circles. "Wait a minute, we never rehearsed."

"Every man for himself," shouts Sophie as she dashes across the street after Ida, plunger at the ready.

Everything seems to happen all at once. The thief dashes out the door of the church, his hands full of bills. He runs right into Ida, knocking the rolling pin out of her hands, but her other hand has the spray can at the ready. She squirts him in the eyes. He stops, momentarily stunned, then twists and turns in agony, rubbing his eyes and stumbling down the stairs. Where he trips over the hem of Sophie's lime green extravaganza and falls down, knocking her down as well.

Meanwhile across the street, Bella is blowing the whistle as hard as her old lungs can manage. With her other hand she is excitedly waving her fly swatter.

Sophie and the thief are entangled as they roll down the steps together. She bats at him with her toilet plunger as they roll. "Get off my gown," she shrieks.

"Help! Help! Someone save me!" the poor-box thief screams. "These lunatics are trying to kill me!"

What a night. It is the big finale everyone has been waiting for: the San Gennaro religious parade and pageant. The floats are gorgeous. Every restaurant on Mulberry Street has outdone itself to be the most grandiose. The neighborhood florists have been emptied of decorations.

Several bands march and play the stately "Triumphal March" from *Aida,* as the religious part of the ceremony, the carrying of the statue of the Patron Saint of Naples that gives the holiday its name, moves slowly down Mulberry Street.

But everyone is waiting for the last float. The news of the capture of the church robber has spread everywhere. Even the *Daily News* and the *Post* have their cameras ready. They eagerly await *La Regina della Festa*.

And here it comes: the biggest and grandest float of all. Sponsored by Ristorante Firenze, the entire float is decorated with poppies otherwise known as white lilics, the national flowers of Italy, and is surrounded by a hundred Italian flags. The huge float is drawn by the Pasquale Funeral Home's polished-to-perfection black hearse. Sitting proudly in the front seat, next to her brother Gino, is Philomena Pasquale, home from the hospital with her entire head bandaged. The hearse itself is crowded with many Pasquales, family quarrels now forgiven.

Sitting high on her throne and wearing her silver tiara is the guest of honor, *La Regina della Festa,* Mrs. Sophie Meyerbeer, visitor from Fort Lauderdale, Florida.

It was decided to pick Sophie to be the queen since she already had a gown (slightly soiled and ripped) with the three colors of the Italian flag: green, white, and red.

Her ladies-in-waiting, Bella and Ida, have dressed up as best they could from their limited travel wardrobe. Sophie smiles down at her sulking "ladies," and whispers, "I told you not to buy those *shmatte*s."

Then she turns grandly to her adoring public, and throws them kisses.

44

PATTY DENNISON

I look around as Jack drives down the main street of Fair Lawn, New Jersey. We are following his exact trip of a week ago.

"The good part is I have you with me this time." Jack pats my knee. He is grinning, I assume, recalling our twenty-minute bedroom almost-adventure.

"If you hadn't been so secretive, I could have done this with you the first time. And stubborn," I add, thinking of how our relationship stalled, and blaming him for it.

He glances over to me. "Truly? Wouldn't you have thought this was an impossible scheme? Besides, I was afraid to drag up your past and make you unhappy. If I failed, I'd never confess; you wouldn't be the worse for it."

I lean my head against his shoulder. "I can't believe I'm actually going to meet Patty again after all this time."

"You're nervous, aren't you?"

"Yes, very."

He gives me a quick kiss on the forehead. "Have courage, my sweet."

Jack turns into the motel parking lot. "We're right on time and so is she. There's Barbara standing next to the blue Ford station wagon."

"You certainly have terrible taste in hotels *and* motels," I say, making jokes in an attempt to cover sweaty palms and a tension headache coming on.

"Hey, I'm a practical man." He grins. "That's a virtue."

I peer out the window. "She's exactly as you described her."

Jack parks the rented Toyota and we get out.

Barbara Sutterfield is skittish. With a cigarette dangling from her mouth, she watches as I move toward her.

"Hello," I say, trying to seem calm.

She examines me for a long moment. "You're the wife." It's not a question. It's as if she needs to verbalize this bizarre reality.

"Yes, I'm Gladys Gold." I almost expect her to ask for proof of identity.

"Patty wants to see you." Barbara doesn't try to hide the fact that she is upset about it, but she's apparently following orders.

Jack doesn't try to pretend to be surprised. "Where is she?"

"I'll show you the way. You'll never find it yourself. You better follow me."

We get back into Jack's rental. Barbara's station wagon is already heading down the highway, not waiting for him. He skids out of the driveway, tires squealing, and catches up to her.

"Touched a nerve with her, didn't I?" I say to Jack. "She must really care about her cousin."

Barbara turns down one deserted dirt road with no street signs after another, churning up dust clouds billowing behind her. Jack's car is covered with it. He can hardly see out of his windshield.

Finally she comes to a stop.

"She was right; we'd never have found this place," Jack comments.

I feel myself tensing up.

We arrive at a run-down farmhouse, small, dingy, dreary, overpowered by woods so dense one would hardly know it was daytime.

Jack and I get out of the car. Barbara backs up until she's parallel to where we stand. She lowers her window; her voice is tight. I can see tears forming in her eyes. "Welcome to the family mansion. I hope you get what you came for." With that she reverses the car and races back down the road, spewing clouds of dust.

For a moment we stare at the house. Jack comments, "Guess it must have been built about a century ago." It's a wreck of a building. Rotted boards. Paint long gone. Torn window shades drawn on every window. Kids would call it a haunted house. And perhaps it is. This is a house of desolation. I don't want to go inside. There can be nothing but pain in there. Anyone who would live inside is not living but merely existing.

Jack and I look at one another. "We can leave now," he says, as if reading my thoughts.

"You know we can't. It's taken this long to arrive at the end of this godforsaken road. There's no turning back."

Jack takes my hand in his. "Whatever is in there ... we have each other...."

No one answers when he knocks. We wait. The door is open. We enter into dimness. Although it's afternoon, it seems like twilight in here. The smells of age and rot assail us. I need to breathe shallowly.

And there she is, walking toward us in the unlit hallway. More like an apparition than someone real. The ghostlike figure turns, and we follow her.

I have the silliest thought that I'm in a Stephen King novel, and in a moment the hall closet might open and reveal a monster made of coat hangers.

Patty Dennison leads us to her old-fashioned, almost primitive kitchen, where there is some light filtering in through the trees into one small window. Now we can see her. She's sixty-three, by my computation. She looks like an eighty-year-old cadaver in a thin shapeless housedress. She wears no shoes. I think of the life I've led, alive and vibrant and living it to my fullest. This is a walking dead woman. Barbara knew it and had wanted to prevent me from seeing what that once eager college girl had become.

Jack tightens his grip on my hand.

Patty wordlessly pours us tea from a kettle that hangs from a slab of iron over a wood-burning fireplace. I don't want to be rude and refuse, but I hate to think about what germs are in that cup. I glance around and I realize I needn't worry. The kitchen, though decrepit, is absolutely spotless and scrubbed. I guess she washes everything with boiling water from the fireplace kettle.

She looks directly into my eyes. "I'm tired of running." The voice sounds dusty from lack of use. She points to an old rickety kitchen chair. I sit gingerly. Jack perches behind me. Patty sits opposite, on the only other chair in the room, sipping her already poured tea.

"Hello, Patty," I say softly. "This is my friend, Jack Langford."

She ignores Jack. It's as if her eyes have fastened themselves only on me. "I know who you are and why you're here." She sips again. "I've thought of you often. Are you well?"

"Yes, thank you, I'm fine."

"Life has been good to you?"

"Yes," I say softly. She's like a fragile glass that might shatter at any moment.

"I'm relieved to hear it. I know you suffered because of me. I'm sorry."

Jack's hands tighten on my shoulders, trying to signal his compassion. I know he is there for me.

I feel I need to reassure her even though I choke on my words. "It wasn't your fault. My husband wouldn't regret that he gave his life to save yours."

"Stop!" Her skinny hand jerks and the tea mug turns over, spilling liquid down onto her clothes and the floor. She pays no attention. She jumps up. "He died for nothing! The bastard who shot him was my boyfriend! Eddie Fitch. I was desperate to be rid of him. I had just told him I never wanted to see him again when he smacked me and knocked me down. I screamed. He warned me if I left him, he'd kill me. And he had the gun to prove it. When Professor Gold came to my rescue, Eddie showed he was serious by shooting him."

So Milt Paxton was right, Jack thinks. All along the girl had known Jack Gold's killer. It was a domestic disturbance, the kind of volatile situation that all cops fear walking into. And Jack

Gold was in the wrong place at the wrong time. My poor Gladdy, to have to find this out.

I gasp. I never expected this. Never. Dear God, help me to deal with this.

"I believed his threats after that," Patty continues. "Eddie said he'd kill my whole family if I ever talked. So I stopped talking altogether."

Jack says softly, "And you ran away."

She pulls her eyes away from me and looks at Jack now. "Yes, to this town where my family came from. Eddie followed me. We never married, but we lived together." She takes a worn rag from the sink, stoops and mops up the spilled tea, and then sits wearily down again. "If you can call that living."

Jack waits. "I'm so sorry."

"He beat me. I worked at the factory to support us. He did nothing but drink and wait for me to come home so he could hit me some more. He terrorized my family. He destroyed all of us. All because I made a stupid error as a kid and picked the wrong guy."

She nervously scrapes her hands back and forth across the bare wooden table. Now, she can no longer look at me, nor I, her.

"Why didn't you call the police?" Jack asks.

"They couldn't help us! I ruined all our lives. My whole family faded away because of him."

She stops, head bowed, lost in her troubled thoughts.

"What happened to him? Where is he now?" Jack asks.

She lifts her head up tiredly. "Finally he got bored with just staying home. He found some gang to hang out with. They robbed a liquor store. I made a phone call and turned him in. He went to prison and within a month, somebody knifed him. He died. I was free at last."

She paused, staring into nothingness. "That was fifteen years ago. It didn't matter. It was too late. I died a long time before that."

We hear a noise. Someone comes into the kitchen. A man of about forty, in old misshapen clothes, shuffles in. There is something wrong with him. He mumbles and is barely able to walk.

Patty gets up and helps him into her chair at the table. She put a bib around his neck and takes out a plate of some kind of soft food from the refrigerator. She stands next to him and patiently feeds him as he listlessly allows her.

"More," he mumbles.

"Our child," she says bitterly. She leans over and gently kisses the blank face. "We share this hell together."

She doesn't look at me or Jack again. I get up.

"I have to leave," I say.

Patty doesn't respond. I can hear her softly humming a nursery song to her son as she forces the food into his flaccid mouth.

Jack and I walk outside and breathe deeply. I watch a tear run down his face. He embraces me. So tightly. I am stiff in his arms.

"I'm so sorry," he says.

I am too numb to cry.

45

PAXTON REVISITED

Jack manages to find his way out of the woods and through the dust-laden, weed-filled dirt roads. He stops the car before turning back onto the highway. We sit there silently. He wants to comfort me, but my rigid body holds him back.

"I don't know what to say."

I shake my head as if to tell him there are no words that will help.

We remain unmoving. I stare out at the desolation around me that fits the way I feel. Not a bird sings. Not a car drives by. It's as if Patty Dennison had moved to the end of the earth to punish herself.

"Are you angry? You should be."

How can I be angry after seeing that pathetic woman? I think ironically to myself. If only she hadn't screamed. If only Jack had come home five minutes earlier. If...if...woulda, coulda, shoulda, as my mother used to say.

"Is there someplace you want to go, Gladdy, dear?"

Again I shake my head.

"Back to Emily's? Get some sleep?"

No. Another head shake.

"Do you want me to drive you to Connecticut to be with Evvie?"

No.

He gives me a wry grin. "There's always 'Pago Pago' at the Dartford. I can order up some mai tais."

I manage a tiny smile. But, no.

I finally speak. I turn to him and look directly at his concerned face. "I feel like I've been on a roller coaster ever since I got here. Seeing you in New York so unexpectedly. Then to find out why you were here. I thought it was all over between us, and now we're on again. Going out to breakfast with you, with all the rekindling of love. And, yes, our precious few minutes in 'Pago Pago.' Then my old neighborhood and this final revelation about my husband's death. My mind is on overload."

"How can you not be?" Jack says. "But I don't know where to take you from here. Where will you feel better? Or find comfort?"

"I have to absorb everything. Now that I have all the pieces."

"Maybe..." Jack starts to say, but stops.

"What?"

"No, you've been through enough. Forget about it."

"Jack, tell me."

"There's another piece. There's another victim in this terrible tragedy. A reporter named Milt Paxton, who was there at the scene when your husband died. I promised him I would tell him the outcome of the visit with Patty."

I think for a few moments. "Take me to him."

"Today? Haven't you had enough? Maybe tomorrow or sometime next week when you've rested?"

"Now, Jack. You mentioned it because somehow you think it will help."

"I could be wrong—maybe it will add more misery to what you already feel. No, I've changed my mind."

"His name jogs my memory. He was there, at the scene, the one who took those photos. He said something to me, but I wasn't able to listen. Maybe he'll remember what he said."

"Gladdy, no..."

"There's no place else I want to go. We might as well."

Jack pulls up in front of Milt Paxton's house in Long Island. The sun is about to make its descent and the air will cool. On the way, Jack fills me in a little about this feisty reporter, Milt Paxton, who lost the use of his legs covering this story.

"That's him. He's still sitting out there on his porch, as if he hasn't moved since the last time I was here. He doesn't look well. His face looks grayer."

"But he seems excited," I say. "I guess when you phoned and told him I was with you he perked up. He sees us."

From his wheelchair, Milt Paxton waves frantically, as if he can't wait another minute until we arrive. We get out of the car and climb the wobbly steps.

"So? So? Tell me?"

"Can't we at least get up on the porch?" Jack leans over and gives him a bear hug.

"Sure, sure, anything." His eyes go to me and he examines me as if with a microscope. "Gladys Gold, it's really you?"

I smile. "Yes, it's me."

His face lights up. "You're a fine-looking woman."

"Thank you."

"So, what do you see in that old guy?" He winks at me and points to the rocker next to him. "Sit. Sit. Here's some lemonade. Don't ask for anything else. My niece took the day off. She thinks she's entitled to it." He grins. "She's a good girl, but I don't ever tell her that."

"How are you feeling?" Jack says.

Milt rattles the newspaper on his lap. "Who

gives a rat's ass about that? I'm still breathing. But not much longer. I'll have a heart attack right now if you don't start talking."

"Listen, Milt . . ."

He slaps at Jack with the paper. "Don't *you* listen? I have been counting the minutes 'til you got here."

Jack teases him gently. "What if I told you there was nothing to tell? That the trip was a waste of our time."

"Then I'd call you a liar. I know you found Dennison. I can see it in your eyes. Don't try to fake a faker. I don't want to hear a crock from you. Sit down, you're making me crazy."

Jack pulls over another chair.

Paxton turns to me. "What is she like, that Patty Dennison? Did she know anything? Was I right, was she lying about what she knew?"

"One thing at a time," Jack says. "Go easy, Gladdy had a very hard day."

"Horse manure. What's with the pompous speech, Mr. Cop? Pardon my language, missus."

"No offense taken." I'm about to speak, but Jack stops me.

"I'm sorry," Jack says, serious now. "I'm here to protect her. First some ground rules. She isn't going to want this case opened again by anyone. And that includes reporters. Not even this reporter."

We haven't discussed it, but Jack is right.

There's no way I'll put myself through that agony again.

"What if I tell you it won't go past me?" Paxton says quickly.

"Then it would be my turn to call you a liar. What about that Pulitzer you've always angled for?"

Milt Paxton half raises himself from his wheelchair. "I don't need no stinkin' Pulitzer," he yelps, parodying the famous *Treasure of the Sierra Madre* line. "I gave my damn legs for this story. I need to know."

"Why, Milt?" I ask. "Why is this so important to you?"

Paxton falls back down in his wheelchair. He takes a deep breath. "So I can finally die."

That shocks me. "You really mean that?"

"Damn it, of course I mean it! I gave all that was left of me for this story. Mrs. Gold, you and your family weren't the only victims. It destroyed me, too."

Jack won't let him off the hook. "Promise not to tell anyone."

"I promise, I promise." He grabs a paring knife from a tray of apples on the small table next to him. "When you're done, I'll slit my wrists. Then you won't have to worry. Better yet, you kill me. It would be a blessing. This is all I'm living for— to know the ending."

"Come on, you drama queen," Jack says, trying to lighten things.

"Come on yourself. You call this a life? My legs are gone. So's my liver from all that rotgut I drank; probably my lungs as well from all the cig butts. My doctor laughs when I come in. 'You still here?' he says."

He laughs so hard, it makes him choke, and then he starts coughing. Jack leans over and slaps him on the back. Finally the coughing subsides. Paxton takes a long drink of lemonade and then grins at Jack.

"Thanks, so tell me everything already from the very beginning, you sadist."

Sunset is over and the sky is showing dark gray and cloudy. Very few stars are seen. Jack starts the narrative and I know I'll probably add to it.

"I went to Fair Lawn last week," he says. "I got a room at a motel and started asking around for Patty Dennison and all I got were hostile stares, so I took out my wallet, figuring a bribe might shake something up...."

Milt Paxton leans back and sighs, a happy man, waiting to hear the story of his lifetime.

By now Milt has us turn on the porch lights; all is black around us except for the lights from his neighbors' houses. Moths dance around the light-bulbs. By now we have removed the lemonade pitcher and glasses, so as not to attract any more bugs. Our storytelling brings Milt up to the entrance of Patty's sad man-child and then our leaving.

For a long while we just sit there, all of us lost in our thoughts. I am beginning to feel better, as if in the telling of the story I've exorcised ghosts. Maybe Milt has also.

I ask him if he remembers what he whispered to me on that terrible New Year's Eve.

Milt Paxton sighs deeply. He nods.

I look at him, hold my breath. "Tell me."

" 'Brave men sometimes have to die. Your husband was a brave man.' That's what I said."

His words choke me up. "Thank you."

Milt shrugs. "Life deals you a hand and you have to play it." He shivers. Jack gets up and places an afghan around his shoulders.

I sigh also. "My husband once told me something when I asked him about what happened to him in the war and he didn't want to talk about it. He said, 'Life goes on with or without your participation. You have two choices: You can wallow in what you can't change, or you can fall in love with the miracle of every day.' "

We sit there quietly. I take the hand of each of these good men and listen to the song of the crickets.

46

GOING HOME

PHONE CALLS:

Evvie to Gladdy: "I can't believe it. Jack's in New York, too? He met your family before you got there? You saw Patty Dennison? How is that possible? How could you not call me sooner? Wait, I can't take this all in on a phone call. I'm coming to the city. I have to hear about *everything*."

Gladdy to Evvie: "Pack your bag and plan to stay with us. We'll leave for the airport from here."

Ida to Gladdy: "You won't believe what's been going on with us. We're in New York. Actually in

Little Italy. Pick up today's *Daily News*. You will be amazed at the adventure we had."

Gladdy to Ida: "You're in New York? How did that happen? Why are you in Little Italy? Never mind, pack all your bags and come up to Emily's apartment. I have to hear all about it. We'll stay here until we leave for home. Evvie's coming, too."

Gladdy to Emily (in person): "Dig up sleeping bags, air mattresses, extra blankets, whatever, from friends, neighbors. You're having company for a few days. We better do some food shopping. We'll need it for the four extra people I've invited."

Emily to Gladdy (horrified): "You've what?"

Gladdy to Emily: "Hey, fair's fair. When you were a kid you used to invite mobs of kids for sleepovers. Did I ever complain?"

Jack to Gladdy: "You're what? All the girls are coming over? I thought..."

Gladdy to Jack: "Just for a few days. Then we can all head back home together."

"I've been making plans. Like moving out of the Dartford roach hotel..."

Gladdy to Jack (interrupting): "Good idea. You can stay with Lisa and her gang 'til we leave."

292 • Rita Lakin

"That's not what I had in mind."

"I know. I know. Well, you can always bring a sleeping bag over and join the nine of us. Ha-ha."

A very long silence. Jack to Gladdy: "Not bloody likely."

Gladdy to Jack: "Love you."

Jack to Gladdy: "Love you, too."

What fun. We're like little kids again. And Bella and Sophie have the mouse pajamas to prove it. Let's face it, when you get old (don't you just hate that word) you enter your second childhood. And believe me, it's more fun the second time around.

We've caught up with everyone's stories. Even my Emily and Alan and Lindsay and Patrick are in stitches hearing the girls' Little Italy adventures—how they saved a woman's life and captured a thief. We read the news stories, show proper delight in their photos on page one, and admire the commendation from the Chamber of Commerce, written in Italian, so that none of us can read it. We are expected to admire Sophie's green gown and watch the choked reactions from Ida and Bella.

However, the kids are purposely not around when I relate my journey with Jack to find out the truth of that faithful birthday, New Year's Eve, so long ago. Everyone is affected by my visit with Patty and its horrendous meaning. Emily hugs me and we shed tears together.

Time to leave, with much promising of returning soon. Jack picks us up in a rented van. To "Jackie's" amusement, he is hugged by all my girls, who now have given him a nickname. My hero.

On the plane, Jack and I manage to sit alone and away from the girls. Not that they don't find excuses to visit.

I can't let go of him. I'm afraid he'll disappear again, even though I know he won't. I clutch him throughout the ride. We cuddle and kiss and say wonderfully silly things to one another. And then I feel as if he hadn't been gone from me at all. I don't know if I can stand all this happiness.

"What are you thinking, Gladdy, dear?"

"Everything. Nothing. Trying to sort out all the crazy things that have happened in so short a time. I thought I had lost you forever."

"Nonsense, you knew you had me with a ring through my nose from the moment you batted your eyelashes and said, 'Hi, I'm Gladdy Gold and I live in Phase Two.'"

I give him a small punch on the shoulder. "I still can't get over it. You had the chutzpah to meet my daughter on your own."

"Ouch, my shoulder is black and blue from all the times you've already hit me."

"And deservedly so."

I hug him again. I never want to stop hugging him.

* * *

The captain announces over the loudspeaker that we are about to land in Fort Lauderdale.

"Jack?"

"Yes, dear. What?"

I inform him. "It's a package deal; you take me, you get four others." I glance down the aisle at my little family.

He sighs. "I can live with that," he says.

The plane touches down at the Fort Lauderdale airport.

I watch as Jack is being driven crazy by the girls as they point out their luggage to him, with Jack lifting one piece of baggage after another off the carousel.

"Jackie, my other one is the powder blue," says Bella, "with the big white pom-poms."

"See it," says "Jackie" patiently.

Sophie grabs his arm. "You missed mine—go run after it. It's the purple one with the yellow flower stickers."

"Not a problem, Sophie, it will come around again."

"I've got my own," says the ever-independent Ida, who will not lean on any man for any reason.

Sophie jumps up and down, pulling on Jack's arm again. "Here it comes again. Don't miss it."

I smile. The patience of a saint. I wonder how long that will last.

As I turn away to hide my laughter, off to one side I see a familiar man's back, through the jostling crowds. He removes a worn, old-fashioned valise off the moving track. I recognize the tweed jacket with patches on the sleeves. He turns around, and there are the horn-rimmed glasses and the unlit pipe balanced in the side of his mouth. We look at one another. The forever-young man and this elderly woman.

"Jack," I say in a gasp.

He grins at me. "It's time," he says, removing the pipe and tipping it in my direction. "It's time to move on."

He lightly swings his bag and heads for the exit as I watch him slowly fade away into memory.

Acknowledgments

About time I acknowledged the wonderful work done by:
Illustrations by Laura Hartman Maestro
Book design by Karin Batten
Cover design by Marietta Anastassatos
Cover art by Hiro Kimura

My great New York team:
Caitlin Alexander
Nancy Yost
Sharon Propson

My great team on the 580:
Camille Minichino
Jonnie Jacobs
Peggy Lucke

Special extra thanks to Camille for San Gennaro

Special thanks to Rose Stone and Barbara Sutterfield for Fair Lawn, New Jersey

And my family and friends for continuous support, you know who you are.

About the Author

Fate (a.k.a., marriage) took Rita Lakin from New York to Los Angeles, where she was seduced by palm trees and movie studios. Over the next twenty years she wrote for television and had every possible job from freelance writer to story editor to staff writer and, finally, producer. She worked on shows such as *Dr. Kildare, Peyton Place, The Mod Squad*, and *Dynasty*, and created her own shows, including *The Rookies, Flamingo Road*, and *Nightingales*. She wrote many movies-of-the-week and miniseries, such as *Death Takes a Holiday, Women in Chains, Strong Medicine*, and *Voices of the Heart*. She has also written the theatrical play *No Language but a Cry* and is the coauthor of *Saturday Night at Grossinger's*, both of which are still being produced across the country. Rita has won awards from the Writers Guild of America, as well as the Mystery Writers of America's Edgar Allan Poe Award and the coveted Avery Hopwood Award from the University of Michigan. She lives in Marin County, California, where she is currently at work on her next mystery starring the indomitable Gladdy Gold. Visit her on the Web at www.ritalakin.com or e-mail her at ritalakin@aol.com.

Dear Reader,

I hope you enjoyed reading GETTING OLD IS TO DIE FOR as much as I enjoyed writing it. And I hope you were pleased with a change of scenery for Gladdy and her girls.

But they are all back home again for their next adventure, and this time, keep your raincoats and umbrellas close by—there's going to be a perilous change in the weather.

Storm clouds are gathering, both in the Florida skies and in the lives of all our beloved characters. Gladdy and Jack will have to put aside their future plans when their condo is hit at the height of a hurricane.

A dead body is found that unearths terrors from an earlier era—and Gladdy and her small band of private eyes must uncover some dreadful truths in time to save the life of someone very close to them.

So watch your local bookstore for the arrival of the new and exciting GETTING OLD IS A DISASTER, coming out next spring. Or go to my website, www.ritalakin.com, to get updates about the arrival of the new books in the series, as well as my schedule of book signings. If I turn up in your neighborhood, please drop by and say hello. And keep those wonderful e-mails coming to me at ritalakin@aol.com. I love hearing from you.

Rita Lakin